Don't Look Back

Jane Donnelly

MAGNUM BOOKS
NEW YORK

Copyright © MCMLXV by
Fleetway Publications Ltd.

PLAYMORE, INC., PUBLISHERS
and WALDMAN PUBLISHING CORP.
New York, New York

Printed in the United States of America

CHAPTER ONE

She didn't look the type of girl you'd expect to see standing beside a tractor. She wore a pink silk blouse, a grey flannel skirt. Her fair hair was straight and fine and long, and her nail varnish was the shade of her blouse without a chip or a scratch to mar it. She looked as though she had stepped straight out of a glossy magazine.

Dozens of men during the last month had stopped, looked appreciatively at the tractor and more appreciatively at the girl, and asked: "Do you go with it?"

Each time she had smiled, as though she had never heard the crack before. "I'm afraid not, but it's still a very good buy."

Kerry Mace was selling tractors. Other farm equipment as well, but tractors took pride of place in this display stand at the agricultural exhibition.

She hadn't known the first thing about them when she was chosen for the job, but she'd learnt facts and figures and now she could chat quite knowledgeably with possible customers before she handed them over to the men who really knew.

Kerry was the glamour. The girl who stood at the front of the stand and smiled and enticed people to stop.

She had enjoyed these three weeks. This was the last and she was going to be sorry to walk out of the great hall on Saturday night. Most of it had been fun, the crowds, the lights, the excitement of helping to make a good sale. There were times when her feet had ached but that hadn't bothered her. The men she was working with, and the men and the girls from the other stands had been a pleasant bunch.

Except for Eric. And he was more nuisance value than a real problem. Eric Morton had been chosen for the same reason as Kerry, because he was good to look at. He gave tone to the display. He was as good-looking as Kerry was pretty, but unfortunately he thought he was irresistible.

She had been dodging him round the tractors since that first morning when he had seen her, opened his eyes very wide, and murmured: "My lucky day!"

"Not on my account it isn't," Kerry had told him. She had gone on telling him with added emphasis, but it hadn't made a scrap of difference. Eric not only wouldn't take "No" for an answer. He wouldn't even be warned off by: "If you make one more grab at me I'll hit you with a shovel."

But Kerry had had experience with wolves. She didn't let Eric worry her. She just side-stepped him and got on with her job.

She saw the tall man coming through the crowds before he saw her and when their eyes met she was surprised to see him stiffen and stare a little. She had had her share of double-takes but this man didn't seem the type. Even less

4

so when she spoke to him. He was a customer. His voice was quiet and unhurried, and he didn't ask whether she was included in the tractor price.

Perhaps it was because Eric was leering at her but she watched the tall man and thought he looked nice. He was in the office now, behind the display stand, discussing farm equipment with Reg. He looked up, and smiled, when he saw her looking at him.

"That your type?" Eric sounded huffy.

Kerry shrugged him away. Might be, she thought, might very well be.

That was how it started. When his business was finished with Reg, the tall man said: "Can you recommend anywhere for lunch?" There were at least half a dozen different eating places scattered around and Reg replied:

"Try the Grill Room. Turn left at the top of the main staircase. Kerry's off duty now, she'll show you."

She wasn't off duty for another ten minutes but Reg was a romantic at heart. He liked Kerry, he liked the way she bubbled with life. He saw them walk off together feeling he had done his good turn for the day, while Eric glared.

Kerry pointed out the Grill Room and had turned towards the staff dining-room when the tall man said: "Won't you have lunch with me?"

He more or less had to say that, she thought, but he sounded as though he meant it and he waited as though her answer mattered.

Kerry usually got on well with people but this time there wasn't even that first five minutes or so of meaningless talk. It really was as though they were old friends. A waiter seated them at a corner table and she asked: "What's your name?" and smiled because she felt she ought to know.

5

"Drury. Garth Drury."

"I'm Kerry Mace."

"That's an unusual name."

"It's really Christina, but everyone calls me Kerry."

He had a slow-growing smile. It started in his eyes before it touched his lips and right from the beginning it did things to Kerry's heart that no other smile had ever done.

Over lunch they swapped life stories. He was a farmer—well who else would want a tractor? He came from Cornwall and he lived with his brother and their aunt. No wife? She held her breath while she asked and when he said: "I'm not married," she relaxed right down to the toes tight-curled in her black high-heeled pumps. If there had been, she had a crazy idea that the brightness would have gone out of the day, the flavour out of the meal.

"Tell me about yourself," he asked. "Where do you work usually?"

"All over the place. I model a little, fashion photographs and I have done a couple of TV commercials."

He looked impressed and she laughed. "Very small fry though. I did have plans to be an actress. I got taken on by a rep. company as assistant stage manager which means general dogsbody, and understudy. But they turned the theatre into a Bingo hall so that was that."

"That was bad luck."

"I suppose it was. Anyhow I don't think I was much good." Kerry was usually honest with herself. "You have to be dedicated to make a first-class actress, I laugh too easily."

She sounded rueful although her eyes danced. She had no complaints. Life was tough but most of the time it had its compensations. Losing your parents when you were only a baby was a bad deal, but Aunt Eleanor and Uncle

Bill had been as good to her as though she was their own daughter. They were in Australia now, they'd gone over to join their son when Uncle Bill retired, and their love still came winging to her.

No, she had no complaints, and certainly not now. Talking, laughing with Garth, the time fled so that when she glanced up at the clock she scrambled to her feet. "I mustn't be late. It's not fair to the others."

"When can I see you again?"

"I don't get any free time until the exhibition's over. We don't close until nine."

"You have a lunch hour?"

"Yes of course."

"Tomorrow then? Same time?"

She ran back to the stand and Eric glared her in. "Have fun with the farmer?"

"Yes, thank you," she said.

Garth came next day. They had lunch together and Eric, eyeing the big man thoughtfully, stopped trying to manoeuvre Kerry into the back office and turned his attention to the girl on the egg packaging display.

At ten past nine when Kerry stepped from the still bright hall into the darkened streets, Garth was waiting for her. She didn't exactly run into his arms but she quickened her pace and he put out a hand to welcome her and it was almost an embrace.

They had coffee and a snack at a little cafe she often used for supper, and Senora Rosa nodded and beamed approval.

Then they walked for a while, and talked. Garth had spent the afternoon touring domestic agencies. His aunt needed help about the farmhouse, but there was no one locally, and he'd had no luck today either. A rambling old farmhouse miles from anywhere wasn't what most domestic helps were looking for.

7

Kerry sympathised. She could imagine the house from Garth's description and she thought it sounded wonderful, but a place like that would be hard to run.

She told him about the rest of her day: the queries, the customers. She had him laughing because even if Kerry would never be a great actress she did have a flair for mimicry. "And bless you for one thing," she said. "I think you've scared Eric off."

"Who's Eric?"

"He's the fair-haired dreamboat on our stand. He thinks he's a ladykiller but after you collected me for lunch he went over and told the girl opposite that he could get her a television test. Up to now he's been telling me."

Garth grinned. "Sounds a very corny line."

"That doesn't bother Eric. He isn't an imaginative lad. Strictly one track."

"I hope the girl opposite knows what she's doing."

"I think so. She sounded as though she did when she was telling me. Eric may end this month wondering if he's losing his grip."

They talked such nonsense but it made the night warm and wonderful, and when she said goodnight to him at the door of her apartment, there was a moment without any laughter at all.

He didn't kiss her, but he held both her hands and she felt the strength of his fingers closing over them.

"Thank you, Kerry," he said. "Tomorrow?"

"Please."

She went upstairs in a daze. Miriam, her room-mate, was sitting cross-legged on her half of the bed-settee putting rollers in her hair. Kerry practically groped for a chair and Miriam hopped up. "Anything the matter?"

"I think I'm in love."

Miriam squeaked, them gurgled with laughter.

"I mean it. Oh, dear, I mean it."

"Why not?" said Miriam, who fell in love on an average of once a month. "It's about time. They've all been in love with you up to now. Now you'll find how the other half lives."

It was a joke of course, Miriam knew it was, but Kerry lay awake into the night, remembering the touch of Garth's fingers and how the lamplight had shadowed his face.

There were so few days left. That was the terrible thing. Only two more before the exhibition closed, and Garth was going home on Sunday.

Saturday lunchtime was rushed. The last day, final orders, a crush of latecomers. There was only time to snatch a sandwich and get back to the job, but Garth was waiting for her when the day ended.

She had said her goodbyes, promising to keep in touch with some of the folk who had been her working colleagues for the past month, and then hurried to meet Garth. Their last evening and she knew it would pass so quickly—so terribly quickly.

She had planned to cook supper in the apartment. Miriam had promised to keep out of the way like Cinderella until midnight, but one gas-ring wasn't much to prepare a meal-to-remember. Soup and sausages were about its limit, and soup and sausages they had.

"You will write?" Garth said.

"Of course."

"And I'll see you again." They had talked about him coming up to town again. They'd been talking about it all evening.

"It might not be London," said Kerry. "I might get a job out of London." She had a piece of sausage speared on a fork. It stayed, poised in mid-air, while she closed her mouth and opened it again. "And why not? You

9

could find me a job couldn't you?''

He didn't understand. "On the farm? It's hard going, a darn' sight too hard for a town girl, and there's nothing else.''

"In the house I mean. Your aunt needs help, doesn't she?''

"You couldn't do domestic work.''

"Of course I could. I'm very domesticated really. Don't let this meal fool you.''

"It's a lonely place.''

"I was born a country girl.''

Suddenly there was something about him—something she couldn't name, a reserve, a withdrawal. She realised that he had never mentioned her going down to Cornwall, not even for a visit. He would come back, that was what he had said. To London or wherever she was. As though for some reason he didn't want her in his home.

CHAPTER TWO

"Forget it," she said quietly. "I'm sorry." She couldn't hide her hurt although she tried, tilting her lips in a smile.

Garth hesitated. He had a cigarette between his fingers and he ground it into the ashtray. "You really meant that?''

"Not if you don't want me to come.''

"But I do." Whatever it was, he had made up his mind. Perhaps she had read more into his reluctance than she need have done. The place was lonely, the house was big, and she did look like an impractical glamour girl. At first it must have seemed a crazy idea to him.

He began to tell her about his aunt who had run the home for him and his brother, Timothy, since they were children

"That's another thing we have in common," said Kerry, "we both have aunts for mothers."

Garth seemed as fond of his Aunt Flora as she was of Aunt Eleanor. You could tell from the sound of his voice.

His voice changed again when he talked about Timothy, still affectionate but now with laughter in it, and Kerry could imagine him ruffling the younger boy's hair, being the big brother, protesting, teasing, sometimes bullying a little.

"I'll love meeting them," she said. Because I love you, she added, keeping these words locked in her heart. Because I want you to ask me to marry you and stay in that house forever.

Less than a week was such a short space to meet a man and know that, but she was quite, quite sure.

It frightened her sometimes, how sure she was, and Miriam for one looked appalled, hearing her plans.

"You're going down there to do cooking and cleaning in an old farmhouse? You're out of your mind. You'll be bored stiff."

"No I won't. I like cooking and cleaning."

"All right. but there's nothing else to do, is there? No one to meet, nowhere to go. It sounds like the end of the world."

Kerry laughed. She was packing, most of her clothes weren't going to be much use. She'd ask Miriam to store some and use those she wanted, they were the same size. She said: "I'd follow him to the end of the world. He doesn't realise it but Garth Drury is a marked man."

Miriam glowered. "I never know whether you're fooling or not. Be serious, can't you?"

"I am serious," said Kerry.

Next day, Sunday, was fine for a car drive. The sun shone and the breeze was light. Miriam, still looking glum, called after them: "Let me know when you're coming back. A postcard will do."

Kerry couldn't feel cross because it was sweet of Miriam to insist that she wouldn't take another roommate. But Garth was looking thoughtful. "She isn't expecting you to be away long."

"She's wrong. I'll stay as long as you need me."

His eyes were grave. "I wonder," he said.

They stopped for lunch at a wayside pub and she wasn't imagining it, Garth was quiet. Something was on his mind and she leaned across impulsively. "What's the matter? Would you rather I went back?"

"Not on your life!" He took her hand across the table and a shiver of excitement ran down her spine.

Cornwall was just as he had described it. They hugged the coastline, skirting the holiday resorts, coming on wilder, lonelier country, going for miles, it seemed to Kerry, without seeing a house. And then at last a little cluster of them and a solitary one here and there.

"Polbryn," said Garth.

"Where's the farm?"

"We're nearly there."

The roads were narrow and twisting, lined by high hedges through which every now and then they glimpsed the sea. A gate and a rough track across the fields led to the grey stone buildings, and by the gate was the name *Norbrook Farm* lashed to a post.

Garth stopped the car, opened the gate. Kerry suddenly felt tense, apprehensive. Because now she would not only see Garth's home and his aunt and his brother, she would find out the reason why he hadn't wanted to bring her here.

The farm was large. They drove slowly because there was mud beneath their wheels, then went under an archway and into a courtyard.

The house door opened and a woman and a young man came out. Kerry wished she could have had a moment to tidy her hair. The open windows had blown it into a tangled mass around her face. Garth had the car door open for her and she stepped out, pushing back her hair with both hands.

She saw the woman stop and falter, the colour draining from her face. She swayed and the young man put an arm around her and said something too quietly for Kerry to hear. As they reached her she said: "I thought it was Miranda."

The name stayed in the air like an echo.

"Didn't you get my telegram?" Garth said.

"A little while ago." The younger man was speaking. He looked something like Garth. You could see they were brothers. There was probably not more than a year or two between them and yet Garth had the authority, the confidence. Timothy looked likeable and kind, but it was easy to see Garth was the head of the household. "Hello!" Tim Drury held out his hand.

His aunt had recovered now. She was pale but composed. She welcomed Kerry, kissed Garth, bustled them both into a huge kitchen where tea was laid on a blue and white checked tablecloth and a fire burned in an inglenook fireplace.

Tea was a mighty meal. Home-made scones and cakes and bread; cold meat to carve; pickles, a great cheese, preserves. Kerry looked at it with wide eyes. She felt she should have complimented Miss Drury on her baking at least, but there was something rather forbidding in the older woman's dignity. Perhaps forbidding was too strong a word, but although she had told Kerry she was

13

glad to see her, and although she was treating her now more like a guest than someone who had come to do a job of work, Kerry sensed a coolness.

Garth told them about the exhibition and the equipment he had ordered. He explained where he'd met Kerry and they turned to her, Tim smiling, Miss Drury with a calm scrutiny.

"Hope you won't find it too quiet down here," said Tim. "We're glad to have you, the work's too much for Aunt Flora, but it's a real backwater, is this."

"I'm sure I won't." She was grateful for his smile, eager to prove she could be as handy as anyone around a house. Perhaps that was worrying Miss Drury.

When the meal ended Kerry got to her feet and began to gather the dishes together. Miss Drury said: "I'll show you your room first."

"Thank you."

"We didn't have much warning but I've had it ready for some time." Garth took up the cases and Tim went on with the table clearing, whistling tunelessly between his teeth.

It was a rambling house, built when families were large and staff easy to come by. The staircase ran away into corridors and corners and there seemed to be doors everywhere.

One swung open a little. It was at the end of a short corridor of its own and Miss Drury clicked her tongue, and moved to close the door. Kerry, immediately behind, presuming this was her room, followed on her heels.

"No!" ordered Garth sharply.

"That was Miranda's room," said Miss Drury. "It isn't used now."

"Who is Miranda?" Kerry asked, turning to them both, but Miss Drury answered her.

"Someone who lived with us for a while." She said no

14

more. Garth said nothing at all, as she turned to another door and opened it.

This room was plainly furnished. There were rugs, not a carpet, on the floor and an old-fashioned patchwork quilt on the bed. The general effect was pleasing and the window looked out over the countryside.

"Get your things unpacked," said Miss Drury, and they left her.

It didn't take long. Kerry put her clothes in the chest-of-drawers that smelt of lavender, or hung them in the deep clothes closet.

It was certainly quiet here but that didn't worry her. There would be enough work in this house to keep two women busy, and she wasn't likely to be bored under any roof that held Garth. Just sitting with him in the evenings, even if she was darning socks and his aunt and brother were sharing the fire with them, would make her happy.

She smiled at herself in the Victorian mirror that swung on its stand on top of the chest of drawers, brushed her hair smooth, and went downstairs again.

Miss Drury was at the sink and Kerry joined her, taking the drying towel. Garth and his brother were looking at letters, accounts. The murmur of their voices was the only sound except for the ticking clock.

Kerry was usually a rather talkative girl. She had questions now she wanted to ask, but Miss Drury, working deftly and competently, was a person who could discourage chatter without any discourtesy.

She was kind. When the washing-up was done she insisted that Kerry should take a comfortable chair. There was a television set and she turned it on, asking Kerry which programmes she preferred. But she kept her distance—there was no immediate offer of friendship here.

Suddenly there was a sound of footsteps in the flagstone corridor outside, and the kitchen door swung open. A young man stepped in, holding a gun and a brace of rabbits. He was wearing corduroy trousers and a rough tweed jacket leather-patched at the elbows. "Back all right then?" he said.

He was facing Garth, who grinned at him. "Did you think you'd got rid of me? Kerry, this is Neil. I've warned you about him."

He hadn't. He'd said that Neil Pontin helped them to run the farm and that he was a nice chap. Neil was solidly built with slightly sandy hair and he flushed a little under Garth's banter. He also stared at Kerry—just for a second she saw the startled widening of the eyes again. Then he said: "How do you do," and he hoped she'd like it down here, and gave Miss Drury the rabbits.

He stayed for supper. They talked farm talk, and after supper Miss Drury got up and said ten o'clock was her bedtime. "I'll give you a call at six in the morning," she told Kerry. "Breakfast at half-past."

"Thank you." Kerry was on her feet too, and Neil Pontin took up his gun and Tim went with him to the door.

For a moment Kerry and Garth were alone. He said: "What do you think of them?"

"They're nice." Then she had to rush on: "Neil stared at me like you did, as though I reminded you of someone. And your aunt thought I was Miranda."

"Yes."

"Who is she? Where is she now?"

Very quietly he answered, "Miranda is dead—she was drowned a year ago."

CHAPTER THREE

There was nothing more she could say, somehow she couldn't pry any deeper. The set of Garth's mouth and the tone of his voice were warnings that she shouldn't. Anyhow Tim was clattering back down the passage still chuckling from some joke he had been swapping with Neil.

She said goodnight to Tim and to Garth. "Sleep well," they both said, and Garth added: "Don't forget it's an old house, boards creak and doors rattle. Don't let it worry you."

"I won't." They smiled at her, and she went upstairs.

Dim lights burned along the corridors, otherwise she might well have lost her way, and she hesitated, glancing down the passage that led to Miranda's room.

Of course she was curious, burning with curiosity. Perhaps later on someone would tell her all about it, but now questions were whirling in her brain.

Had Miranda been a relative or just working here? There was no reason why Garth should have mentioned her when he was talking about his aunt and Tim, yet why hadn't he? The tragedy, obviously, was vivid in their minds. It was strange that there was sucn a strong likeness between herself and Miranda that Miss Drury had looked near to fainting.

She went into her room and got ready for bed. You could hear the sea. Perhaps it was only the wind but it sounded like the sea. She snuggled deeper between the sheets and drew them up to her ears trying to shut out the sound. But she heard it all night, even in her dreams.

In her dreams a girl's voice mingled with it, sometimes singing, sometimes calling.

She was awake when Miss Drury came into her room and stood for a moment looking down at her. "Did you sleep well?"

"Very, thank you." It wasn't quite true but it was a small lie, and Garth's aunt smiled as though she was relieved to hear it.

"I've been listening to the sea," said Kerry. "You can hear it very clearly. Almost as though it's lapping round the house."

"Yes." A curious expression touched the older woman's face. "Sometimes it does seem very near." She went out of the room, closing the door quietly.

Flora Drury wasn't a demanding employer. She was plainly glad to have Kerry, the work was far too much for one not-so-young woman, and surprised to see Kerry tackle cooking the breakfast with so little flurry.

"You know your way about a kitchen," she admitted.

"I should. My aunt's a marvellous cook. She brought me up and she never did hold with idle hands." Miss Drury's smile reflected Kerry's infectious grin.

The men ate their meal and went out into the cool morning. Kerry had never seen Garth in working clothes before. In town he looked like a man-of-the-world, his suits expensive and well tailored. Now he was in breeches and a black polo-necked sweater and she thought he looked even more handsome.

She wondered if he would kiss her goodbye, but perhaps that was too much to expect with his aunt and brother looking on. Anyway he didn't. He smiled at her and said: "Don't let Aunt Flora work you to death. She's a slave driver," with an affectionate wink for his aunt who glared at them and smiled too.

"Let me show you the rest of the house," she said as

soon as the men had gone. "We don't use it all now. If I show you the ones we're trying to keep up, you'll know what kind of job you've taken on."

They still covered a fair area, but a good half of the house was shrouded by dust sheets. Kerry wondered if Miranda's room was. Miss Drury didn't open that door, nor refer to it again. She showed her own room, Garth's, Tim's, a couple of spare bedrooms. Downstairs, besides the big kitchen which seemed to be the main living-room, there was a study, a dining and a drawing-room.

In all the rooms the furniture was much the same: heavy, solid and good. Victorian without being too ornate, and with here and there touches that were almost startling. Like the writing-table in the window of the study. That was Georgian, a lovely fragile thing. And the picture in the drawing-room, a pastel of smudged blues and pinks, very Parisian against the oil paintings in their heavy frames.

She helped to turn out the drawing-room, and enjoyed herself. It was a satisfying house to work in, spacious, away from the grime and dust of cities.

When the men came in for their midday meal and the women doled out braised steak and dumplings Kerry could almost believe she had been doing this all her life. They ate together, Neil Pontin had most of his meals with them, Miss Drury had told her.

It was pleasant. Tim, who had a boyish sense of humour, was ribbing Neil about someone called "Lissy," and Neil was blushing and grinning sheepishly.

"You'll meet her tonight," Garth told Kerry. "We'll take you down to the White Bear and you can see her. Put in a good word for Neil if you get the chance."

Lissy turned out to be the barmaid. The White Bear was the local pub, the only one for miles around, and in the evenings it was more like a club for the men and women who lived in the rather isolated village.

Not for Flora Drury. She belonged to a generation when ladies never went into "licensed premises," but she agreed with Garth and Tim that they must take Kerry along to meet the folk.

Kerry was delighted, she wanted to make friends with Garth's friends. She put on a sage green skirt and a soft coral coloured sweater, and walked between the brothers along the winding lanes into the road leading down to the bay. That was the village. The pub was roughly halfway down, and so small that you would have passed it as another house if there hadn't been a swinging sign of a chained bear outside.

The people inside were waiting. A new face was an event here and they had been told she was coming and had turned up to see her. That was the impression Kerry got. She didn't resent it, it was understandable, but by now she was expecting that flicker of recognition and she saw it, time and again.

She longed to ask: "In what way was Miranda so like me? Eyes? Hair? The shape of her nose? Tell me about Miranda."

But nobody spoke the name. Instead they hoped she'd be happy here and the girls asked her to tea. The only work, apart from another couple of farms, was the sea. The men were fishermen, and they looked it with their tanned skins and strong hands. The women looked like fishermen's wives and daughters, eyeing Kerry's clothes and complexion with rather wistful envy.

They were nice people. Anyone, Kerry felt, could be happy living among them. She was sure she could. Everyone was on Christian name terms from the start. Vic, Denis, Rawley, Trix and Mary.

Lissy, behind the bar, had red hair and bright eyes and was thrilled to hear that Kerry had been in a TV commercial and in a few magazines. She swore she had seen pictures of her, but Kerry felt that was just kindness.

The Trelawneys were particularly friendly. Roland looked like a pirate with a big black beard, and his wife was pretty and plump and dimpled. They ran a guest house at the top of the hill.

"Well, not really a guest house," said Shirley Trelawney, "but I used to be a nurse before I married and even if we are off the beaten track the place is very healthy. I suppose it's more a convalescent home in a very small way."

Kerry could imagine her and Roland being kind and considerate hosts. She said so and Shirley smiled. "Thank you. For that you can come up to the Crow's Nest any time and I'll nurse you for free. By the way, you're settling in all right at Norbrook?" Her voice had changed. The banter had gone out of it.

"Yes, thank you," said Kerry. "It's a big place but most of it's closed up so it won't need too much attention."

"I wasn't thinking of the work." Shirley had a drink in a long-stemmed glass. She twisted it slowly between her fingers. Denis was playing the piano, most of the others gathered round him.

Shirley said: "Remember, you can come to us any time."

"Thank you." Kerry sounded a little bewildered. There was so obviously an undercurrent of meaning to this.

"Norbrook's a strange house," Shirley went on. "Don't ask me why, for goodness' sake, but just remember, come when you need us."

She laughed across at someone who had called out to her and Kerry was left to wonder if she really had said that, because it didn't seem to make any sense.

The rest of the evening went like a typical get-together of friends, and when everyone said goodbye and Kerry turned for home, her hand through Garth's arm, she had a nice warm feeling. Everyone had made her welcome.

She should have felt light-hearted, and she did except for the shadow of Shirley's words. "When you need us," Shirley had said. "Not "if" but "when," as though there was no doubt that the time would come when something or someone at Norbrook Farm would send Kerry running for help.

Did she mean Aunt Flora? There was reserve there but, if Kerry was any judge, nothing underhand or hurtful.

Surely not Tim. Certainly not Garth. Then who? What? Why had Shirley Trelawney looked at her with more than pity in her eyes, as though there was something fearful, unspeakable, ahead?

CHAPTER FOUR

In the big kitchen of the farmhouse the fire burned brightly, brasses gleamed on the mantelpiece, willow pattern plates on the Dutch dresser. Miss Drury sat knitting by the fire, and she looked up with a welcoming smile.

Everything seemed ordinary and safe, but beyond the doorway of the kitchen was the hall and the staircase and all those closed rooms and unlit corridors. And the silences were filled with the sound of the sea.

As she lay in bed that night, Kerry told herself she was getting too imaginative by half. Shirley Trelawney hadn't meant anything more than, "Come and see us any time, we're always around."

"Norbrook's a strange house," she had said, well, so it was. Old and rambling, and as Garth had told her, full of creaks and shiftings. If she didn't know it was only the old boards she could almost believe that soft feet were pattering up and down outside her door.

All the lights were out, everyone had gone to bed ages ago, and here she was lying, listening. And for what, for goodness' sake?

It took willpower to make herself relax. She thought of Garth and how perfect it was to be here with him, and at last the tiredness of her body won and she fell asleep.

She awoke before Miss Drury called her. She was up and dressed when the tap came on the door.

They were already falling into a routine. Breakfast was cooked, served, cleared away, the rest of the day's meals planned. There was no popping out to the shops here because there were no shops. All the supplies were brought in each Saturday from a nearby larger village. But there were rooms to be cleaned, plenty to do.

Kerry chattered as she worked. If you were going to live in the same house as another woman you had to tell her things about yourself. Even if she was quiet and didn't tell you much in return.

Maybe there was nothing to tell. Flora Drury had lived here all her life. Like her brother she had been born in this house. Garth and Tim loved her, and because of this Kerry could have loved her too, but there was still that air of aloofness about her, even when she was smiling. And sometimes Kerry felt that there was pity in her eyes.

But the days went happily enough, everyone was kind. On Thursday she went to tea with Mrs. Lovelace, who had a house almost at the sea's edge, piles of nets in her kitchen and the salt smell of fish over everything.

Beth Lovelace, and Nat her husband, were twenty years older than Kerry but they made her feel at home,

23

and asked her about life in London and wondered how long she was going to stay in Polbryn.

"Not many people come here," said Beth. "Most of us have lived hereabouts all our lives. Shirley's the one who comes from the farthest distance and she's Cornish stock. I don't think we've had an outsider ever." She wasn't being hostile, just stating facts. "Of course there was Miranda," she added, slowly.

Nat had been stuffing tobacco into his pipe, his shoulders hunched. Beth sat with her hands in her lap, and Kerry had the feeling that their thoughts were dark. She said quietly: "Miranda who lived at Norbrook?"

"Yes."

"Was she a relative?" This felt a little like disloyalty, prying behind Garth's back, but she had to know.

Beth shook her head. "No, she stayed with the Drurys, helping Flora, the same as you're doing."

"It must have been dreadful." Kerry meant the tragedy of her death, of course, but they both turned and waited as though they were not quite sure what she meant. She blundered on: "Garth told me she was drowned."

"Yes, oh yes, that was what happened." Beth sounded almost eager. "The currents are treacherous round here you know. It was a terrible thing."

Kerry wanted to hear more but Beth was telling about Ian, their son, who was at the university. She was fetching out snapshots and letters, a little feverishly as though the moment must be filled.

No one wanted to talk about Miranda. Kerry learned that during the next couple of weeks, and she also learned that no one had forgotten her.

She thought at first that it was Miss Drury's little whim that nothing should be moved about the house. Every chair, every vase, had to be replaced in exactly the same

24

spot. Once Kerry shifted the little bureau a fraction nearer the window and Miss Drury put it back. Another time she bought an armful of chrysanthemums when they were shopping on Saturday. At least Garth bought them for her, and she found a vase and arranged them while the family were out of the room.

Tim came in as she was standing back, admiring. "There, aren't they pretty?" she said. "They're the first of the season and they smell wonderful."

He said: "Oh Lord, where did you get the bowl?"

"Off the little table in the drawing-room."

"You'd better not use that one. I'll get you another."

She didn't mind, although it seemed odd. "Why?" she asked.

"It was Miranda's bowl. She said it was never to have anything in it but yellow roses. They were her favourite flowers."

Kerry wouldn't have expected Tim to remember a thing like that, though the bowl usually did have yellow roses in it. Miss Drury attended to them herself. Kerry said: "Was your aunt very fond of Miranda?"

"Yes."

Perhaps that was why she was so guarded with Kerry. She had given her affection to another young girl and that girl had died. She still missed her, or she wouldn't be putting yellow roses in the blue bowl. Perhaps when she saw Kerry about the house it reminded her painfully of Miranda.

"How do I look like Miranda?" she demanded.

Tim didn't want to talk about it. He shifted restlessly, then said: "Your hair. She had long fair hair like yours."

Kerry touched it. When Miranda was in the sea it must have floated like flaxen seaweed, she thought. "How long was she here?"

"About six months. Let's get something for those

25

flowers." She was being snubbed, he didn't want to talk any more about Miranda.

Neither did the others. Kerry went several times with Garth and Tim to the White Bear, and now she was greeted like a friend, but all the time they were waiting for something.

She couldn't have said how she knew. She read it in quick, almost furtive glances, in their voices when they said: "Everything all right then?"

Nothing tangible, nothing to put a finger on, but they were waiting for something to happen.

The weather was breaking. Up till now it had been fine and warm, but for the last two days clouds had sculled across the sky and the sea had looked grey and sullen.

Not that Kerry saw much of the sea. While she was working she was indoors, and if they didn't go round to the White Bear in the evenings, or sit at home watching television, Garth would drive her out for a meal or a cinema somewhere.

Those were the best times of all, when she was alone with Garth. Then she knew that it hadn't been infatuation although it had been so sudden and surprising. The more she knew him, the more she found him strong and wonderful, and the surer she was that before long he would ask her to marry him.

They weren't lovers, except in the lightest of ways. The kiss, the arm around her shoulders, consideration and kindness. All that she got from him, but she didn't fool herself that his blood raced as hers did when they stood close.

It would have taken so little for Kerry to admit that she was passionately in love. Garth wasn't. Garth had his feet firmly on the ground. There was no wild music in his blood, but one day, Kerry promised herself, one day you'll hear it as loud and as clear as I do.

26

"We're in for a storm," he said, as they drove home. The film had been a comedy, only a fair one but Kerry was happy, her head on his shoulder.

The sky was starless, and so heavy that everything seemed muffled by a black blanket. Thunder rumbled as they parked the car in one of the barns that served as a garage, and a flash of lightning cut through the sky. Kerry ran as the first drops of rain fell.

"We just made it!" Tim, Neil and Miss Drury were in the kitchen. She laughed at them. It had been a near thing, the rain was pelting down now. Then she realised that no one had smiled back, their faces were set, almost grim.

As Garth came in Neil said: "Miranda weather."

"Yes." Garth went to the coffee pot on the hob and poured a cup for Kerry, another for himself. "If it keeps up you're going to get soaked walking home. You'd better stay."

Perhaps it was because this house was so exposed, high on the hills overlooking the sea, that the storm seemed to explode around them. Rain was lashing the windows, thunder rolled and lightning flashed, and Kerry asked a little morosely: "Do you often have it as bad as this?"

"This is storm country," Garth told her. "It sounds worse than it is. Well Neil, if you're staying, how about a game of chess?"

They did sometimes play together. Miss Drury occasionally played patience with ivory yellow cards. She took out her pack now and said: "We might as well go into the drawing-room."

A fire was laid and flared at the touch of a match, and somehow in this room the noise of the storm seemed to be less. Perhaps it was because of the carpets and the thick velvet curtains drawn across the windows. Kerry sat by the fire reading a magazine that Shirley had lent her, and

27

Tim wrote a letter, and all the time the thunder echoed around the house.

Tim seemed the most restless of them all. Several times he put down his pen to get up and wander around the room. He stood behind Garth's chair, criticising the moves of both players until Neil said: "Drop it, will you? I know what I'm doing."

"What's for supper?" Tim wanted to know.

"Cold ham in the pantry, some pickles," his aunt said.

"I'll get it." Kerry jumped up and Tim trailed along behind her. In the kitchen he helped her carve the ham, cut the bread.

Lightning flashed even through the gingham curtains and she flinched. "I've never known such a storm!"

"You just don't notice them the same way inland."

She said, suddenly: "Neil said it was Miranda weather. Whad did he mean?"

Tim had gone to the window. He pulled the curtains aside now and looked out into the raging night. "Miranda liked storms. I've never known anyone else who enjoyed them as she did. She came in a storm and she went in a storm."

Kerry waited, hardly breathing. It was almost as though Tim had forgotten she was there although he went on talking to her. "Her father's ship was wrecked just off the coast, the rocks are bad there. It was a cabin-cruiser and he was drowned, but she got ashore. She was pretty shaken up but Aunt Flora and Shirley nursed her for a while and afterwards she stayed on."

He paused. "Then there was a storm the night she died."

"What happened?" Kerry whispered.

"She was drowned. She shouldn't have been near the sea on a night like that, but she loved storms. We used to tease her, call it Miranda weather, we couldn't keep her

28

in. Funny that, you'd have thought after her father's boat had gone down in a storm she'd have been scared of them, but she wasn't."

He let the curtain fall. "Do you believe in mermaids, Kerry? Neither do I, but sometimes I used to think that's what Miranda was."

It didn't sound like Tim talking. He seemed to realise it. He rubbed the back of his hand across his eyes and laughed in an embarrassed way. "Let's get on with supper."

The storm lasted into the early hours but after a while Kerry's ears became accustomed to it and she did manage to sleep. She wondered how the others were faring.

Miranda weather. Every time there was a storm they would remember Miranda, her coming, the way of her death, the days and nights between when she had gone out into the rain and the wind laughing because she loved storms.

Then Kerry slept and when she woke it could have been the final rumblings of thunder she heard. She wasn't sure and she lay still. Some alien sound had plucked her from sleep, and now there was nothing but the dying storm.

She sat up in bed, peering around. There was nothing to see but the shape of furniture, and then she caught a breath of perfume. Sharp and sweet. She had never used or encountered it before, but it was a perfume that a girl might choose and make her very own.

"Who is it?" Kerry whispered. "Who's there?"

CHAPTER FIVE

No one answered. Of course they didn't, she was alone. She felt foolish, hearing her own voice, but for all that she reached for the light switch and the room became bright.

Now she wasn't sure about the perfume either. She sniffed and there was only a faint scent from the lavender bags in the drawers and cupboards. Perhaps it had been the end of a dream. Some dreams did spill and she waited for sleep again, but it took a long time to come.

Next morning everything looked washed out, trees and fields and buildings still dripping from the downpour, the sky a flat grey. It was as though nature had exhausted herself in the force of the storm and Kerry thought that no one looked as if they'd had a particularly good night's sleep. They ate breakfast in subdued fashion, and when the three men went out to start their work in the fields Miss Drury still sat at the table.

Kerry had almost finished clearing before she looked up. "Are you all right?" Kerry asked anxiously.

"I didn't sleep too well."

"The storm was certainly noisy."

"You sleep well, don't you? There are often noises in old houses and you're not used to them yet. You mustn't let them disturb you, it's something to do with the structure getting warped after so many years."

"So Garth said." Suddenly she had to add: "I woke last night, perhaps that was why."

"Yes." Miss Drury sounded breathless. "Yes, it would be."

"I thought I could smell perfume."

Now there was no mistaking the alarm in the older woman's eyes. She was still sitting in her chair, and she gripped the wooden arms until her knuckles gleamed. "What kind of perfume?"

"It's hard to describe a scent. Floral I suppose, but not sweet, a sharp scent."

Slowly Flora Drury got up and walked to the Dutch dresser. She opened a drawer and took out a little bottle. It had no label. It was the sort of container you might buy from the chemist's. She unstoppered it and held it towards Kerry. "Like this?"

"That was it! It's lovely. What is it?"

"Just scent. A pharmacist, a friend of ours, made it up." She replaced the stopper and the bottle. She came back to the table and sat down again. "For Miranda," she said.

Kerry stood very still. "No one else uses it?"

"Not that I know of."

"But it was in my room last night."

"Scents cling. Haven't you noticed that? For months, years sometimes. Perhaps some was spilt in your room, a little of it would linger."

She kept her eyes on Kerry's face, level and challenging. They were faded now but once they must have been very blue. Kerry nodded. "Of course. That must have been what happened."

The day went on. They did their work and neither of them spoke of it again, but Kerry couldn't keep down a niggling doubt, because surely in twelve months there would be no sign of a splash of spilt perfume, and last night she had smelt it as clearly as though the girl wearing it had stood there, near enough to touch her.

The mail came late that day, the storm had made the lanes hard to negotiate, and the postman's boots were

31

heavy with mud when he did put in an appearance. He stayed for a cup of tea and put down a handful of letters.

Those for Garth were mainly business ones. There was a knitting pattern that Miss Drury had ordered from a newspaper, an airmail for Kerry from Aunt Eleanor, and a thick envelope for Tim.

The postman grinned, handing that over. "Due back this week, isn't she?"

"That's right. Tim's counting the days."

The letter was from Clare. Kerry had been told about her. She lived in Polbryn and worked in the next village teaching at the infants' school. For the summer holidays she had gone hiking all over Italy with another teacher, and her brightly coloured postcards had been coming for Tim by every post.

Kerry was looking forward to meeting her. She sounded quite a girl.

Their next visitor that day was Shirley Trelawney. She came on a bicycle, her hair blown by the wind. "What a night!" she said. "Wasn't it wild? I thought the roof was going once or twice. How did you get on?"

"We're still here, as you see." Miss Drury spoke before Kerry could say anything, and again Kerry was left with the impression that there was something behind the question.

If she said: "I woke and there was perfume in my room," she wondered whether Shirley would be surprised, or whether she might even guess what perfume it was.

"I came to ask a favour," said Shirley. "My Betsy's had an accident." Betsy was someone who cycled in from the next village twice a week to give Shirley a hand. The Crow's Nest was a small house compared with the farm, but it was just about as inconvenient as it could be, built on three storeys, and all the rooms at the oddest angles.

32

"It would happen now," Shirley went on, "she was going home when the storm caught her and she skidded into the ditch. They think she's broken her ankle."

Everyone sympathised, both with Betsy and with Shirley because, after a month with no guests at all, she was expecting several in the next few seeks.

"Isn't it just the way?" she grumbled. "Anyhow, I wondered whether there was any chance of you giving me a hand, Kerry? Even one afternoon a week would be a godsend."

Miss Drury looked at Kerry. "It's entirely up to you."

"I'd like to," said Kerry. Shirley was fun to be with, her bubbly nature was a tonic, probably that was why she had made such a good nurse. And if Kerry could help, of course she wanted to.

They settled that she should go over the next morning and Shirley departed on her bicycle.

Kerry didn't regret her offer. A morning in the Crow's Nest was like a coffee date with the girls back in the old days.

They worked, of course. Betsy hadn't been much of a one for cleaning under beds, or anywhere else that was out of sight. Kerry and Shirley did a good morning's cleaning, and then settled down to a pot of coffee and a plate of soft, spicy buns, while Shirley looked at the horoscopes in the newspaper.

She herself was promised: *Good news money-wise,* and launched into plans of how she would spend it, starting with a suit she had seen in a newspaper. Though that would have been less than no use at all at Polbryn.

"What are you?" she asked Kerry.

"Virgo. September the twelfth."

Shirley read aloud: "Something has been worrying you lately, but the outlook is brighter." You could always twist a horoscope to fit in with your wishes or moods.

But Shirley leaned forward. "Has something been worrying you?"

"No. Well," Kerry hesitated, "a little. You started it really, that first evening when you said I might need a friend, when you said Norbrook was a strange house."

"Yes?" Shirley denied nothing. She just sat there, grave, waiting.

"On the night of the storm something woke me. At least I think it did. I woke up and lay there, I didn't hear anything but there was a distinct perfume."

Shirley began to stir her coffee, the little spoon clinking against the sides of the cup.

"It was a perfume Miranda had specially made for her," Kerry said.

Shirley nodded. "I remember."

"Could a scent linger in the air for twelve months?"

"I very much doubt it."

"Tell me," Kerry said, "why is everybody scared when her name crops up? The accident was a dreadful thing, but there's more than that, isn't there?" Shirley bit her lip and Kerry repeated: "Isn't there?" again and louder.

"Folk say they've seen her." Shirley couldn't mean it the way it sounded, but a coldness crept through Kerry. "On the cliffs and in the cove. Especially when there's a storm."

"Since she *died,* you mean? But that can't be true. You know it can't. Who says they saw her?"

Shirley said quietly: "Jock Weathersgill, for one."

Kerry was shocked and speechless. Jock was the landlord of the White Bear and a man she would have described as practical through and through. If he saw a shadow, or a trick of moonlight, or a strange shaped rock, he'd know. He wouldn't mistake it for anything but what it was.

She could only gasp: "Jock says he saw Miranda?"

34

"Not only Jock. I could name you a dozen others."

She did. Fishermen who had sailed by the cove and seen a white figure running to and fro at the water's edge, or standing on the cliff looking across at them. Folk crossing the moor. Names of people Kerry knew.

"It can't be true. They must have been mistaken," she said.

"All of them?"

"There has to be an explanation."

"Why?" Shirley spoke grimly. "Maybe we're country yokels down here and you town folk are smarter. We still have witches, you know. Some of the old folk still believe in the little people. Strange things can happen in lonely places like this, and some of them have no explanation."

Kerry stared at her incredulously. "You really believe that Miranda haunts the place where she died?"

"I haven't seen her. I've only been told."

"But you believe it?"

"I wouldn't go near that cave after dark. I know that much. Any more than I'd live at Norbrook Farm, because she's there, too. Can you honestly say you haven't felt it yourself?"

CHAPTER SIX

Kerry came back with her mind in a whirl. She didn't know whether to laugh or argue. It couldn't be anything else but superstition and yet men like Jock, and women like Shirley, a practical, unfanciful, fully-trained nurse, believed it.

Shirley had only sat there, sipping her coffee, while Kerry protested that of course she had no reason for thinking that Miranda was still at the farm. The perfume could be explained, scents *did* linger, and there was absolutely nothing else.

But all the time she was remembering those soft footsteps in the corridor, the door of Miranda's room open when all the other doors were closed. Even the yellow roses. She knew that her voice was shrill because she was trying to reassure herself more than Shirley, and Shirley said nothing at all, until Kerry faltered into silence.

Then Shirley said: "You asked me. I told you."

"But it's nonsense, crazy."

"Yes," Shirley agreed, "isn't it?"

Kerry walked back to the farm hardly knowing what to do next. You couldn't forget a thing like this. You had to talk about it, ask about it. Garth and Tim and Miss Drury knew. They had tried to keep it from her, warning her that any noises she heard would only be the creakings of the old house. They had expected noises. Miss Drury hadn't been surprised about the perfume, either.

There was no one in the kitchen and she went upstairs to her room, taking off her coat, trying to compose herself. You had to stay sane and reasonable when you heard something as far-fetched as this. In London you'd smile and have a dozen explanations ready, but in this house with its closed doors and twisting passages and the sound of the sea everywhere, you weren't sure any more.

She saw her reflection in the mirror, the fine fair hair, and she tensed as though she expected the features to change until she was looking at a strange face, another girl.

Miss Drury must be around somewhere. She never left the house empty. Probably she was in one of the bedrooms.

Kerry came out of her room and turned slowly to face the little corridor that ended in Miranda's door. It was ajar. Perhaps there was something wrong with the latch, and no matter how often they closed it, next time you went upstairs it was open again.

Kerry walked towards it. She had shut the door before, but never opened it, or looked in. It was one of the rooms that wasn't used, there was enough work with those that were, that was the only reason. But was it? Or had she never looked into Miranda's room because she was afraid of what she might find there? This was getting out of hand. She was working herself into a state of nerves. Her fingers closed round the knob and she pushed the door, slowly.

She knew then for sure that the touches that had seemed out of place in the rooms below had been Miranda's. This furniture was like that bureau in the drawing-room. There was a table and a bow-fronted chest of drawers that could have been made by the same Georgian craftsman. Carpets, walls and curtains, were the pastels of the painting. It was a beautiful room and someone had chosen everything in it with care and pleasure and a great deal of money.

Kerry saw all this in a fleeting glance, and then the one thing that wiped everything else from her mind. A dress hung on a hanger hooked on to the wardrobe. Miranda must have been very slim, average height, but slim. The dress was white, threaded with silver, long and fitting. A bride's dress.

"You're back," said Miss Drury.

She stood in the doorway and Kerry turned to her. "Who was Miranda going to marry?"

"Garth."

She had known that. Right from the beginning she had known that Miranda meant more to Garth than just a girl who had worked for his aunt and met a tragic death. The natural thing would have been to ask him about Miranda

37

weeks ago, instead of learning a little here and a little there.

That first evening, the only time she had spoken of Miranda to him, his eyes had warned her. She hadn't admitted it, even to herself, but she knew now that she had never asked again because she was afraid he might say: "I loved her."

"Close the door," Miss Drury said. "I'll make you some tea." There was kindness in her voice. "Shirley Trelawney told you, I suppose, that's why you came to Miranda's room."

"Yes."

"I thought she would. She's a great talker. Has it frightened you? Do you want to leave us?"

"I don't want to leave. It can't be true."

Flora Drury walked on ahead, downstairs to the kitchen. The kettle was singing on the hob and she took down the tea caddy. "It's true," she said.

"You mean you've seen her?"

"No, but I could. Most days I could. Go upstairs alone and you can feel her behind you. I've heard her footsteps and the rustle of her skirt and smelled that perfume she used. I don't look back. If I did I know she'd be there at the end of the corridor or coming out of her room."

"No!" Kerry whispered. "This is madness."

"Do you think I'm mad?" Miss Drury smiled, her lips firm in her strong face, her eyes sharp and clear.

"Of course not, but you've got to be mistaken."

"Move anything, from the way it was when Miranda was alive and she'll put it back again. She like things just so. In some ways she was wild. She loved storms and sailing and riding over the moors, but in the house nothing had to be out of place." She sounded indulgent as though she was humouring a much-loved child, and Kerry's heart ached for her.

"You were very fond of her?"

"She was a lovely girl."

"And Garth was going to marry her." She made herself say it even though the words hurt.

Miss Drury nodded. "He took it worst of all, of course. He still can't talk about her. When we're together, Tim and I do, often, but never if Garth's there." She looked at Kerry pleadingly. "I suppose you'll tell Garth what Shirley told you?"

"What good would it do?"

"None at all, but if you feel you have to talk about it with him I can't stop you."

"What do you want me to do?"

"You're a sensible girl—most would have been in hysterics by now. I want you to carry on as usual. She won't hurt you. Everyone knows that, although they keep away from the cove at nights and not many of them would care to move in here."

It wasn't the easiest thing to do. Kerry's instincts were to ask everyone she saw if they believed it. She needed reassurance but she didn't think she was going to get it from the folk who lived round Polbyrn. And she didn't want to talk to Garth about it.

Of course she didn't believe it, but for all that she found it harder now to accept that the noises were only the house's noises; and she left Miranda's door still slightly open. What was the use of closing it when it always opened again? Besides, for some reason, she didn't like touching it.

She wasn't seeing much of Garth these days. It was harvest-time. The storm had done some damage but they were still harvesting a fairly good crop and everyone was at work until the last glimmering of daylight. When he came home he was bone-weary, with no energy left for going out.

Kerry understood, of course. She did all she could to see that their food was ready for them, and most days she turned out too and did a few hours of less heavy work. She enjoyed that. It was fun.

And Tim's Clare came home. He introduced her to Kerry the first evening and they liked each other on sight.

Clare Heard was almost beautiful, a slim tall girl with grave dark eyes. Not that she was dull. She was up-to-the minute and go-ahead, and when she laughed her eyes sparkled.

Like Kerry, the harvest was playing havoc with her social life. Tim was as busy as Garth, and most evenings Clare would bring a pile of school work round to the farm and wait for the brothers to come in.

Kerry could always find plenty to do. She was cutting out a dress one evening when Miss Drury had gone to spend the evening with a friend, and the two girls had the kitchen to themselves.

Clare dropped a book on the flagstoned floor and Kerry jumped so that the scissors leapt out of her fingers.

"Sorry," said Clare.

"Nerves," Kerry smiled. "I never knew I had any until I came here and heard the local tales."

"You have heard?"

No one had said any more after Shirley Trelawney.

"I've heard we're supposed to be haunted." She went on smiling, but Clare didn't smile.

"I've seen her," she said.

"Miranda? Where?"

"In the cove. I think Tim and I were the first. We went out one evening quite late, after I'd been here to supper. I knew that odd things were happening at the farm, Tim told me, but I wondered if Aunt Flora was imagining half of them, for she was very fond of Miranda. And then Tim and I saw her.

40

"She was at the water's edge. I saw her hair and the dress she was wearing."

"What happened?"

"A cloud went over the moon and she'd gone."

Clare spoke simply and there was no doubting her sincerity. She said: "Why do you stay here? We don't talk about it, if we did there'd be research teams down here, sensation seekers. We'd be over-run. If anyone from outside did start asking questions everybody would deny everything. But we all know that there's evil about. Why don't you go back to London?"

"Why do you come each night?"

Clare smiled ruefully. "Because I'm in love with Tim."

"Maybe I'm in love, too."

"Not with Garth?" Clare's voice was quick with alarm. "I know you're good friends but don't fall in love with him. You mustn't, because he's still Miranda's. He'll never belong to anyone else."

CHAPTER SEVEN

The pain was like a knife-thrust. Of course Clare was wrong. But it was horrible to hear, like someone telling you that you would never see another spring. One day Garth had to love her. He was the one man, the only man, all her hopes and her dreams were of him.

She remembered his kisses. Those first days when he had spent every moment he could in her company. And since she had come down here he had taken her out as often as he could. There was an understanding between them, but he had never told her he loved her.

Perhaps it was only friendship as far as he was concerned. She felt sick and cold but Clare could be right. The memory of Miranda could be so deep in Garth that no other girl would stand a chance.

Clare was looking at her, her dark eyes wide with concern, and Kerry said: "Did you like her?"

"Yes."

"Everyone seems to have. She must have been a wonderful person."

"Not wonderful, but she did have charm."

"You don't think Garth will ever forget her?"

"For a long time he wouldn't believe she was dead. He knew but he couldn't accept it. I don't know whether he accepts it even now."

Kerry said wildly: "The door of her room's always open."

"I know, and have you ever smelt the perfume?"

Kerry nodded.

"I don't believe in ghosts," went on Clare, "but I saw Miranda, and she's in this house too. You can *hear* her upstairs." Then, abruptly: "They never found her."

"What do you mean?"

"Some of her clothes were washed up. It was a rough night, the sea could easily have torn them off, but her body was never found."

"You don't think she's still alive?"

"No, of course not. If she was, she wouldn't be wandering in the cove at dead of night or hiding in this house. She isn't physically here, that's for sure, because once we searched—Tim and Neil and I. Something had happened."

"What?"

"There was the farmers' dance coming up. It's a county affair, quite a big do, and we were trying to persuade Garth to come along. Tim said something about there being lots of pretty girls, you know the sort of thing Tim would say. Garth wasn't keen and we were trying to persuade him.

"Aunt Flora was in bed with a chill and I took her a hot drink." Clare had an exercise book on her knees and as she spoke she looked down at the round childish print almost as though she was reading her words. "The door of Miranda's room was wide open, not like it usually is, but wide so that I could see the bed. There was a dress on it, the one Miranda had worn at the farmers' dance the year before, and a pair of gold shoes. I dropped the glass." Clare seemed a little ashamed of that. "It slid right through my fingers and I started to shake as if I were going to fall to pieces. Kerry, she was getting ready for the dance! That's how it looked.

"I went downstairs and I told them. Garth didn't say a word, he just walked right out of the house and I don't know where he went. We didn't see him for hours. That's when we searched—we went through this house from top to bottom, cellars, attics, everything. There was no one there." Clare was shivering now.

Kerry said: "I still have to stay, even if she's listening outside the door." She was angry with herself for saying that, practically admitting that the stories were true.

Not that Clare had lied, but rumours could grow so easily. All right, so there was a girl in the cove one night, with fair hair, and Tim and Clare had decided it was Miranda. There was no proof. It could have been someone like themselves, walking along the coast. She might not even have been alone. It was a cloudy night and their eyes were only for the light-clad figure. Once seen, anyone who glimpsed anybody in the vicinity of that cove would be sure they'd seen Miranda.

And here in the house Miss Drury was missing her, as much as Garth perhaps, because Miranda had been with her all day and every day; and old people were fanciful.

Forgetful too. Miranda's room was dust-free so Miss Drury obviously cleaned it, taking clothes from the cupboard from time to time. She had put that dance dress on the bed and then forgotten about it.

There were such simple explanations. Kerry clung to them in the days that followed.

Clare had been right about Garth. Kerry watched and saw it. Before, his silences and his quiet moments had just been Garth and she hadn't intruded on them. But now she knew what his thoughts were and she watched for the shadows that touched his face, the darkening of his eyes.

She wanted, more than anything in the world, to beg: "Talk to me about her. Tell me." But the words wouldn't come.

Life seemed to go on normally. Routine was now established at the farm, and twice a week Kerry went over to the Crow's Nest to spend the morning with Shirley.

Shirley didn't talk about Miranda again, any more than Clare did. Kerry had a suspicion that they both felt they had said too much already. Miranda was a shameful secret.

Kerry's outings with Garth started again; now they were often foursomes with Tim and Clare. On those evenings when they all piled into the car together, Kerry thought that no one would believe they were anything but a party of light-hearted young folk without a real care in the world.

Garth was a wonderful companion. So was Tim, but Garth had the quiet authority which always got them prompt service. They had their favourite eating places. Kerry was introduced to them, and it was all very pleasant. Except that she knew they had done this before with Miranda.

Sometimes they met people who looked hard at Kerry,

obviously remembering Miranda.

She became used to it. She considered having her hair cut, but an almost tear-stained letter from Aunt Eleanor stopped her. It had been Aunt Eleanor's pride, and when Kerry casually mentioned that she thought she'd have it cut very short Aunt Eleanor's letter zinged back by return post.

Kerry hadn't talked about Miranda in her letters. She had said that they believed in ghosts around here, and pixies and witches, but she'd made it light and amusing. Once she started going into details she knew that her emotions would have shown through, uneasiness, fear. Of course there was fear, she woke sometimes cowering with it. If Aunt Eleanor and Uncle Bill knew they would be really worried.

For Aunt Eleanor's sake she kept her hair as it was.

She was cleaning the bedrooms when she found the rose. It was Garth's room and the rose was on the table, a just opening bud of creamy yellow.

She picked it up and a thorn jabbed her so that when Miss Drury looked in a few seconds later, from making the bed in Tim's room next door, Kerry was sucking her thumb.

"What have you done?"

Kerry held out the thumb and a spot of blood oozed from it. "That rose?" said Miss Drury. "Give it to me." She took it from Kerry and placed it gently on the table again.

"Do you think that's fair?" Kerry said quietly.

"What do you mean?"

"Miranda liked yellow roses. That's why we still have them in the drawing-room. I don't think you should put them in Garth's room, too. We should be helping him to forget, not remember."

"My dear, I didn't bring the rose in here."

45

"Garth did?"

"Perhaps he did."

Did that mean that after they came home last night he had thought of Miranda, had needed a symbol of her through the dark hours?

Kerry wondered whether Garth saw more than any of them. "Don't look back," Miss Drury had said. "She won't hurt you," and although Tim didn't say it in words he meant the same.

But did Garth look back? If he caught that breath of perfume, as Kerry had caught it more than once, did he wait? Did he turn when there was the faintest sound behind him? If he heard those steps in the night did he open the door, and was there a girl there with fair hair and a yellow rose between her fingers?

Kerry knew that this had to end. She couldn't bear it any longer. She didn't believe it was helping Garth in any way to keep up a conspiracy of silence. No one spoke to him about Miranda because it would hurt him, but surely hurt, kept tight and secret, was the most savage of all.

Perhaps it would estrange him from her for ever, but she had to do it, because being with him now was like being with a man who lived a double life. She couldn't help him if he kept her locked out in this way.

She was scared. For days she knew what she was going to do and put it off. She nearly asked advice, from Clare, or Shirley or Miss Drury, but she could guess what they'd say. They would stop her and that wouldn't be hard. At least Garth liked her now, his eyes were warm and affectionate when he looked at her. What if they became cold?

That night Tim and Clare had gone out on their own. The television was dull and Flora Drury was dozing in front of the fire, her book slipping from her knee.

Garth smiled across at Kerry. "Would you like a walk?"

It was a clear bright night, and they were all nodding in this warm room. "Yes," she said eagerly.

She went upstairs to put on a coat and tie a scarf around her head. She didn't look at Miranda's door although she was sure it was open again. She hurried, fastening the scarf as she came downstairs, buttoning her coat in the hall.

Garth was standing waiting for her. They went out into the courtyard. "Any particular direction?" he asked.

"Let's go along the coast."

"Fair enough." That was over rough ground, there was no proper path just here, and the sound of the breakers grew louder as they climbed towards the cliffs.

Down below, rocks rose from the black foaming water, and you could just see the shape of the cove.

"Don't get too near the edge," Garth put out a hand and it was the touch of it, the longing and the loneliness it stirred in her, that gave her courage.

She said: "Was this Miranda's cove?"

He didn't answer at once. She couldn't raise her head. She watched the white-edged rocks and thought how cruel they looked. Then he said: "No, just round the bay, over the hill."

"I've never been there." She made herself turn to him but his face looked as hard as the rocks. "Was she cut off by the tide? They're treacherous round here, aren't they?"

"Why do you want to know? Just idle curiosity?"

"*No!* Please don't think that. It's because we're friends and I want to help. She's still in your mind. I'm not supposed to talk to you about her but I think it would help to talk. She's locked in with you and I—" She faltered. She couldn't find the words. She couldn't say, "I am locked out and I'm afraid of those memories. I'm afraid of your silence when it means Miranda."

47

She could only say desperately: "We are freinds."

He said gently: "There are some things that even friends can't help. And the way Miranda died is one of them. She wasn't caught by the tide. She wasn't on the beach that night. She threw herself from the cliffs down on to the rocks and it was my fault."

CHAPTER EIGHT

"I don't believe it." Her own words seemed to echo in her head. She had been saying that again and again since she came to Norbrook Farm. "I don't believe . . ."

There was no emotion in Garth's voice. He sounded very tired.

"What happened?" The wind blew her words away.

"We quarrelled and when I left her she called after me: "Goodbye, Garth, you'll be sorry. Goodbye."

"That doesn't mean anything. It could still have been an accident."

"I don't think so. It was a wretched night, there was a storm, and she'd insisted on going out in it. She nearly always went to the cliffs over the particular cove. There are some stones that make a sort of rough shelter and she used to sit in that. I'd been out on business and when I got home she still wasn't back so I set out to find her. We'd had a brush that morning, there'd been a dance the night before and like a fool I'd been jealous. Every man there seemed to want to dance with her. It was nothing really but somehow it flared up again. I suppose I was wet through and fed up, and she wouldn't come back home.

"I couldn't tell you how it happened but suddenly it wasn't an argument any more. We were saying things that—" He bit his lip. He could remember every word, Kerry knew, and she knew that he tortured himself again and again, recalling them.

She said: "A girl wouldn't kill herself over a quarrel."

"Miranda might have. She was—oh God, like the storm, willful, impulsive. She could have jumped off the cliff."

"You loved her?"

"Of course I loved her." What a food she'd been to ask. She couldn't take any more just now but at least she had broken the silence of his reserve. No memory of Miranda could hurt him more than her death and the way she had died. Later, perhaps, he would be able to talk of other things. Psychiatrists believed that talking freed you and Kerry would listen, even if he told her what Clare had said, that no other woman could ever take Miranda's place.

But now she could only say: "Shall we go back home?" and take his arm and try to draw him gently away.

He came from the edge of the cliff and perhaps she imagined that when he half turned his head he was listening to the sound of the sea as though it was a voice, calling him.

Garth had to be made to believe that Miranda had died by accident. As long as he thought he was the cause of her death he would carry guilt with him, would never forget her.

She said so to Clare, who was helping her to make coffee. She frowned at the boiling milk. She and Tim had been back when Garth and Kerry returned, and now everyone but the two girls was in the drawing-room. Kerry told Clare where they had been and what she had done, and Clare said: "Why?"

"He needs to talk about it. You must know that keeping your trouble to yourself makes them worse."

"Yes, I know," said Clare.

Kerry wondered aloud: "If they never found her, how did they know she fell down the cliff?"

"Someone heard her scream. Edgar, he's another farmer, was going home and he heard her. He got help and they went to look and there was a strip of her dress caught on a jagged piece of rock halfway down."

It was like a jigsaw puzzle, every piece reluctantly given. Slowly Kerry was piecing the picture together. It was ugly and frightening. But at least Garth had told her.

She said: "I'm sure I was right to broach the subject. He didn't bite my head off. I know the worst now."

"Do you?" said Clare. She poured the milk into a tall jug. "I still think you should have left it alone."

"Would you if it were Tim?"

Clare didn't answer until the last drop of milk was poured. She put the saucepan into the sink and turned the tap on it. With her back to Kerry she said: "If it were Tim it would break my heart because I should know that I didn't have a chance."

"I won't accept that!" Kerry's lips were set and mutinous. It would have been easy to let them tremble and her eyes fill with tears. She didn't feel either sure or strong. But she had always been a fighter and she loved Garth so deeply.

"You're going to be hurt," Clare said gently.

"It doesn't matter."

"Oh, my dear!" She put an arm around Kerry in helpless affection. "I wish I could help you. But I can only keep on saying—leave him alone. And you're not going to listen to me, are you?"

There were footsteps outside the door and Tim walked

in. He looked from Clare to Kerry. Clare shook her head fiercely and Kerry turned away. She had to. She needed those few seconds to compose herself, before she could smile and pretend that everything was all right.

She didn't know what Tim thought or what Clare would tell him, but somehow she felt that Clare would protect her. There was integrity about Clare that would stop her betraying a confidence, even to Tim . . .

Next day was Kerry's twentieth birthday. She hadn't told them and when she awoke she had a lonely feeling. It was the only time she had ever woken on a birthday morning with knowing that someone would burst into the room singing *Happy Birthday*.

Last year she had been with Miriam and they had had a party and filled the apartment with noisy friends. There had been a boy in love with Kerry, who sat all evening watching her. She had thought it was a joke, but now she was ashamed of her laughter and callousness. Love wasn't funny, not even an infatuation that cooled quickly. It could hurt, oh God, how it could hurt!

It had hurt Garth, even when Miranda was alive. He had been jealous because all the men wanted to dance with her. Kerry tried to shut out the picture, by jumping out of bed, washing, dressing and hurrying downstairs. She was often up first now, and had the kettle boiling when Miss Drury arrived.

At breakfast Garth showed no signs of the grim and pain-wracked man who had looked from the cliffs on to the rocks. He was self-controlled again, discussing the day ahead with Tim.

During the hour or so last night with Tim and Clare and Aut Flora, drinking coffee, sitting round the drawing-room fire, he had been so silent that his aunt had looked concerned. She hadn't said anything, but Kerry knew she was worrying about him and it made her feel guilty. It was her fault. She had made Garth talk.

Now he smiled at her as he went out with Tim, and she wasn't sure whether to be glad or sorry. She wanted him to smile, but did it mean he intended to pretend last night hadn't happened, to shut her out again from his heart?

The postman came when she was alone in the kitchen. There were birthday cards and a couple of parcels, and she took them up to her room. Miriam had sent stockings, another girl a bottle of scent, and there was a letter from Aunt Eleanor saying that a parcel was on the way. Tomorrow she would tell them here. Tomorrow they wouldn't feel they had to dash out and buy presents for her.

The day went uneventfully—it didn't feel like a birthday. She stayed longer than usual at the Crow's Nest because Shirley was expecting a guest the next day and there were last-minute arrangements to be made.

Kerry enjoyed the company. Shirley was always good fun and Roland, her husband, had a dry, sardonic sense of humour. The guest, he told Kerry, had been to them before. She was a semi-invalid who, once or twice a year, proved too much for her long-suffering relatives and was shipped off to the Crow's Nest.

"They pay very well," he sounded rueful, "and they need to, my lovely, because she is a dragon. Miss Elvira Lambert. Remember to dodge her."

"She keeps to her room," Shirley protested. "If she wandered around I don't think I could stand her myself. But the money is good."

It was late afternoon before Kerry and Shirley were through, and Shirley said: "I'll walk back with you, I want to see Miss Drury."

It wasn't far, a car passed them, but they saw no one else. The house looked very quiet, without a light or a movement in it.

Often, walking up to it, Kerry wondered what she would do if she saw a curtain flutter and a girl with hair like her own looking down at her. Would she run, hurry to the room? Or would she close her eyes and turn her head, as she was certain the rest of the villagers would? All but Garth, perhaps. She felt that Garth would run, calling a name, begging the girl to wait until he reached her.

There was no sound as they opened the door and walked along the passage to the kitchen. "Miss Drury," Kerry called. "I'm back."

She opened the door and the room was full of people. She gasped at them. Everyone seemed to be there, the whole of the village. True, it was a very small village, but thirty-odd folk can make quite a crowd in one kitchen.

"Happy birthday to you . . ." they sang, and Kerry blinked because tears had sprung to her eyes. How did they know?

Shirley was laughing and pushing her in. "You thought I'd forgotten, didn't you? You told me your birthday when we were looking at horoscopes, but you thought I'd forgotten."

"Shirley, but how sweet of you."

The table was laden, a cake in the middle with one large candle. "We didn't want to embarrass you by going into details," Clare was teasing her. "When a girl gets to our age . . ."

Somehow they had arranged this today. It must have been part of the plan that Shirley should ask her to stay longer. Miss Drury must have been baking all day. Even with help she could hardly have had time to draw breath since Kerry left that morning.

Flora Drury was never demonstrative. Sometimes Kerry had wondered if Garth's aunt secretly resented her taking Miranda's place. Not in Garth's affections, perhaps, but around the house, doing the things Miranda used to do. Being alive when Miranda was dead.

But this birthday party, surely, must mean she was fond of Kerry, whether it was a thank-you for the work Kerry did, or a gesture of friendship. Surprise and happiness choked her so that she couldn't get out a word. She threw her arms around Flora and kissed her.

The older woman smiled. "A very happy birthday to you, my dear."

"But look at me, just look." Kerry was in her working clothes. She had fixed her hair and her face a little before she left Shirley's but not enough for a party. "I must change," she panicked.

"Five minutes only," warned Garth.

Clare went with her to see she took no longer and Kerry hurried into a dress, feeling as excited as if she were ten years old.

It was a very good party. When they went into the drawing-room Neil took flashbulb photographs with the enthusiasm of the amateur who believes in keeping a record of everything. Practically everyone had brought her a present. Clare's and Tim's was a bracelet, a thick gilt chain hanging with lumps of coloured glass, ruby red, emerald green, sapphire blue. Miss Drury's was a pair of gloves and Garth's a stole.

The stole was beautiful, Indian and hand-made, heavy embroidery on wild silk, with silver and gold thread catching the light. It was almost too lovely to wear. Kerry put it around her shoulders and felt like a princess.

She was wearing it when the last of the guests waved goodbye and only the family and Clare remained. It was so late that Clare was staying overnight.

"We'll leave this till morning," Flora said, nodding at the jetsam of the party, and everyone agreed, realising how tired they were and how late it was.

54

Kerry slept at once. She didn't even dream. She lay in deep and happy slumber until fingers of light fell across her face and she stirred and moved luxuriously.

She had hung her stole over a chair at the bottom of her bed, where she could see it as soon as she opened her eyes. She blinked now, trying to focus on it.

It wasn't there! It must have slipped to the floor. She swung herself out of bed to get it.

There was no stole. The chair stood on the rug and beneath it was nothing but one long, green strand of seaweed.

CHAPTER NINE

Her eyes wide with disbelief, Kerry stood for a long time. At least it seemed a long time. Again she wanted to clap hands to her ears and scream, "I don't believe it," but the stole had gone and the seaweed was there.

She stooped and picked up the strand of seaweed and it was clammy cold so that she dropped it again.

"Clare," she thought. "I must tell Clare."

She ran along the empty corridor to the spare room where Clare was sleeping. The door wasn't locked. Clare was sound asleep, her dark hair a cloud on the pillow, and Kerry touched her shoulder.

She woke at once, eyes wide in terror, then recognised Kerry and went limp with relief. "Good grief, you scared me!"

Kerry didn't ask why. She knew. She said: "My stole's gone, the one Garth gave me."

"You're sure?"

"I'm sure. And there was a piece of seaweed on the floor."

Clare closed her eyes and her face was pale. "I thought about Miranda last night, she loved parties. What are we going to do?"

"I want my stole. Garth gave it to me and I want it." She sounded like a stubborn child, but it was the first real present he had given her and it was such a beautiful thing. She said suddenly: "Will you come with me to her room?"

Clare got out of bed, but slowly and reluctantly. She slipped her coat over her shoulders. "All right," she said.

Kerry couldn't have said what she expected to find. The stole perhaps, tossed on the bed or hidden in a drawer. Not to find the room so cold and so empty, without even a hint of that perfume.

She went to the chest of drawers and opened them, but there was tissue paper over each drawer. Nothing had been disturbed here for a long time.

She said wildly: "It wouldn't be a joke, would it?"

"No." Clare spoke with finality.

"I'm going crazy. I'm really asking myself if a girl who's been dead a year came into my bedroom tonight and took my stole."

"I know."

"Well, tell me she didn't. Tell me I'm crazy."

"I don't know," said Clare, and her own voice was ragged. "You tell me who else would take it."

"It isn't here. Will you come with me?"

It was lighter now, but cold and grey and very early. Clare shivered. "Do you mean to the cove?"

"Yes."

"Shall we call Tim and Garth?"

"Tim if you like, I'd rather not tell Garth." That was why she hadn't run to him. Even in those first moments of blind panic she hadn't wanted Garth to know that Miranda resented his gift. He might have said: "Leave it, forget it," and that would mean: "Let Miranda keep it. She mustn't be hurt. Your loss doesn't matter."

Kerry dressed feverishly, and then the two girls went to Clare's room and she too scrambled into her clothes.

"There has to be an explanation, even if it's that I've been walking in my sleep," Kerry said. "I did once as a child. Only once, but I suppose I might do it again. I don't believe in Miranda's ghost. I don't believe in ghosts of any sort. I have to go to the cove to prove that to myself. Do you understand?"

They were outside now, walking quickly away from the house. "Yes," said Clare. "You're like me. Your mind says no, but still you're scared. And after you've spent as long as I have searching for a logical explanation you'll still be left as I was."

"How?"

"I saw her. No explanation fits that. She walked along by the sea just six weeks after she died."

This was Kerry's first sight of the cove. As Garth had said it was over the hill, around the bay. They reached it in twenty minutes and began to scramble down towards the beach.

The cliffs fell almost sheer except for this one track, and Kerry had to look up at the highest cliff. Against the sky-line she could see the outline of several tall stones. "They made a round shelter," Garth had said, "she used to sit there." It was near the edge. She would only need to take half a dozen running steps and then she would fall, arms wide, dress billowing to catch and tear on that jutting crag, and down to the rocks and the sea.

Kerry crouched, sick and dizzy, and Clare said: "I never come here now. No one does."

The tide had gone out, leaving rock pools and smooth

sand between the shingle and the boulders. The bay wasn't large. You could see in the sea pointed rocks like a barrier reef, and it was easy to understand how Miranda's father's ship had gone down and why this was wrecker country in the old days.

With a gasp Clare stopped dead and pointed. Kerry's stole lay on the beach where the tide must have left it, dirty and limp as a rag. Kerry reached it first and picked it up, and shivered to see how it was torn. Surely the sea hadn't done that, rending it to ribbons as though a knife had slashed it?

Clare said in a voice that Kerry didn't recognise: "She had long nails. I used to wonder how she kept them so long."

"Let's go back," was all Kerry said.

They were silent all the way. Kerry could feel the wet silk deep in her pocket. Clare had her hands in her pockets too and her shoulders hunched as though the wind was cold. It wasn't. There was no wind.

Miss Drury shouldn't have been up. The clock said ten to six, but she sat at the kitchen table, an untouched cup of tea before her. "Did you go for an early walk?" she asked. Her manner was the deliberately bright one of somebody pretending all is well and knowing it isn't.

Kerry dragged the stole from her pocket, and put it on the table, and Flora Drury said heavily: "Where was it?"

"Thrown up by the sea, on the beach."

"Yes, it would be."

"Did you *know*?"

"I should have done. I've been worried in case she became jealous of you."

Miranda could have been in the next room, or upstairs, dressing for the day, coming down any moment to join them.

"She's dead," Kerry said pleadingly. "You know that.

58

She can't be jealous." She tried to talk gently but she felt on the verge of hysteria.

"She shouldn't be," said Miss Drury. "She knows that no one will take her place. We're fond of you for yourself, not because you're replacing Miranda."

Was it a warning, Kerry wondered? Garth is for no woman. Garth is for her.

Clare said: "Life has to go on, Aunt Flora. The rest of us have to go on living."

"Of course we do, my dear." She sounded as though Clare had said something very obvious. "And we mustn't worry. Miranda will understand that Kerry doesn't mean to hurt her."

She picked up the ruined stole and put it into a cupboard under the sink. "We'll get rid of that later. Garth mustn't see it."

The men came down, and there was breakfast to serve and eat before they went out to their work, and Clare had to leave to catch the bus. No one mentioned the stole, or that the girls had been down to the cove.

Yet somehow Kerry half-suspected that Garth knew. He seemed thoughtful. Tim did most of the talking, but then Tim usually did. When they said goodbye Garth held her hand and looked at her closely and she knew that she was still pale. It had been a late night and a good party, perhaps he would think that was the reason. "All right, Kerry?" he asked.

"Of course."

"Bye then." He kissed her cheek lightly, and he and Tim went and she and Clare faced each other.

"We didn't tell them," said Clare. "Why didn't we? Because Aunt Flora didn't want Garth to be worried?"

Miss Drury had walked with the two men into the courtyard. She was out of earshot.

"No," said Kerry, "not just that." She knew she was

talking nonsense. "Miranda wants **him** to know. And I'm not helping her by telling him."

Clare spoke slowly. "You sound as though you've accepted her, as though you believe in her now."

"I don't!" She said it fiercely. "I won't! But you said it, didn't you? Who else would have resented Garth giving me a present?"

Flora Drury came back and Clare put on her coat and said goodbye.

There was work enough today. All the debris of the party to clear. Kerry said again: "It was so kind of you. The party was a wonderful surprise."

"Nonsense, my dear, you're good to me and it was a very little thing. Besides," when she smiled you realised she must have been a very pretty girl, "we have to make our own pleasures here, our own excitement, and everyone enjoys a party."

Excitement! thought Kerry. They believe that a dead girl moves among them and she talks of excitement! She haunts the cove so they keep away. She's in this house so you don't look back in case you see her.

Flora Drury said gently: "You're still upset about your stole. It was naughty of her."

"How can you be so calm about it?"

"What do you mean?" She sounded as though she really didn't understand and Kerry found herself stammering:

"Things like this don't happen."

"But they do. They always have."

"Oh, people believed in ghosts hundreds of years ago, just like they believed in witches. But not now. Things have changed."

Flora Drury was smiling, tolerantly. "No, my dear. We pretend they've changed, that's all. You've lived in cities. They muffle the senses. You'd even forgotten the sound of a storm until you came here.

"You know the sort of countryside this is. It feeds us and clothes us but we have to fight it and love it and live close to it. And the sea. More people have died on those murderous rocks out there than anyone will ever know. We've lived with ghosts for generations."

She made it sound so simple that Kerry was left without a word to say, as though she was the one who was being superstitious and silly, and Miss Drury was talking commonsense.

She turned back to her work. Several women looked in, to help with the clearing up, to say how much they'd enjoyed the party.

Shirley came with the news that Miss Lambert had arrived. "She hasn't improved a bit." She grimaced as though she'd bitten on a lemon. "Sour old thing. She's sitting up in her room, ringing for attendance as though we'd got a staff of fifty. Sometimes I wonder if we didn't make a mistake opening a convalescent home instead of an ordinary guest house. We do get the most difficult types."

Aunt Flora chuckled and Shirley cycled off, warning Kerry that she would probably refuse to set foot in the Crow's Nest again after one brush with Elvira Lambert.

"I won't say a word," Kerry laughed. "You can tell her I'm the village idiot."

That evening Neil brought his photographs. They were still damp and tacky from the developer, but they were very good. Kerry had seen other photographs he had taken. She had learned something about photography in her modelling days and it was obvious he had talent.

These were well worth keeping. There was Kerry cutting the cake; Clare biting into a king-size sausage roll; groups galore.

She stiffened as she picked up the next one. It was a

close-up of Garth putting the stole around her shoulders. He looked tender, affectionate; and the camera had caught vividly Kerry's look of overwhelming delight at the gift.

Quickly, she slipped it beneath the others. It was almost as though she wanted to hide it—before Miranda could see the dawning love in their eyes.

CHAPTER TEN

Neil stayed to supper, as he usually did. He and Kerry talked about photography techniques, and he said: "You must come down to the cottage and see some of my other stuff. I've had some accepted for exhibitions."

So Garth had told her. "Thank you," she said.

"I like portraits best. I've done some quite good ones."

Tim had gone out with Clare. Aunt Flora was in the kitchen, and Garth wasn't in the room. Kerry said quietly: "Did you do a portrait of Miranda?"

Like Tim, like Clare, like all of them, his eyes clouded. His "Yes" came out reluctantly,

"You have it?"

"Yes."

"I'd like to see that," she said. "I'd like to see Miranda."

But she knew already what Miranda would look like. She felt she would have known her, recognised her in the street if they had met . . .

She went along to Neil's cottage next day. The walls were covered with photographs. Some were scenes of moorlands, the cliffs and the sea, but most were portraits.

They really were extraordinarily good. There was one of Flora Drury, showing her strength of character more clearly than any words could have described it, although she was only standing at her front door, hands loosely clasped before her. There were studies of fishermen, dragging in their nets; of Garth and Tim at work on the farm. Everybody in the village had been snapped by Neil at some time or other, and he took Kerry round, proudly pointing them out.

But she had to ask him again before he showed her Miranda. He took the photograph from a drawer and laid it slowly on the table.

Miranda, sitting on a rock, hair blown around her, had made a beautiful picture. She was very lovely. Her eyes were huge and dark, her features elfin. She looked like the waif who would turn into a princess, like a mermaid, as Tim had said.

Kerry thought: No one would ever forget her. No man who had loved this girl would ever stop remembering.

She said: "Do you believe in ghosts, Neil?" That wasn't fair. He coloured and looked acutely uncomfortable.

"I don't know."

"Everyone else here does. They all believe that Miranda's still at Norbrook in that room of hers, following Miss Drury and me around, putting the ornaments straight." Heaven knew she wasn't making a joke of it. It was no joke, although her voice was flippant.

"I don't know," Neil said again, and put the photograph away, and she felt a little guilty for having embarrassed him.

She said: "Thank you for showing them to me. I think they're all very good indeed and that one in particular."

He smiled. "I'm glad you like it."

"She was beautiful."

"Garth saved her life, you know. When the cabin cruiser hit the rocks he got her out. We thought she was dead, she was so limp and white, but we gave her artificial respiration, and then we took her to Norbrook, and Shirley and Miss Drury nursed her. It's cruel to think that after all she had so little time. She should have married Garth and lived here until she was an old woman. That's the way it ought to have been."

Kerry felt it again. Whether they told her in honest words like Clare, or obliquely like most of the others, they were warning her that Garth belonged to Miranda. Even Neil looked sorry for her while he spoke.

She thanked him again and he walked back to the farm with her, and they all wanted to know which of the photographs she'd liked best.

She said: "The one of you, Miss Drury, is awfully good."

Aunt Flora nodded. "It is, isn't it? He's a clever lad."

They discussed Neil's pictures for a while, but no one asked if she had seen Miranda's photograph, and neither Neil nor Kerry mentioned it.

Sometimes, of course, she wondered if they were right, and there was no hope at all for her. Garth was unfailingly kind and considerate. When he came in from the fields, midday and evening, he looked for Kerry at once and his eyes warmed at the sight of her.

When he touched her, no matter how fleeting or impersonal the contact, her heart pounded; and she knew that she was going to love this man and no other for the rest of her life.

But there was Miranda. Even if there was no ghost she was in Garth's mind and in his heart. Should she leave, Kerry wondered, go back to town and pick up the threads of her old life? Miriam was writing regularly, the apartment was still waiting, friends still asked after her.

She even had offers of jobs. Her agent wrote that he might be able to get her a part in a children's TV serial if she'd turn up for the audition. It wasn't the chance of a life-time. She'd only have been in one or two installments, but before she met Garth it would have sent her rushing for the nearest telephone. Now, she tore up the letter.

When she faced things calmly she knew she ought to go, there was so much here that was strange, terrifying. Beneath the surface there were shadows as dark as madness. And yet she stayed, doing the hundred and one dull little daily tasks: peeling potatoes, making beds, discussing recipes with Shirley and Beth, hairstyles with Lissy, the barmaid at the White Bear, gossip with Clare.

With the sound of the sea always in her ears, and never daring to glance over her shoulder when she was alone.

She stayed because of Garth. Because of a tall, dark man, with a quiet voice and a slow smile, who was so right for her in every way but one. And that one was called Miranda.

Shirley had been right about Miss Lambert. Kerry didn't see the woman for some time. She went round to Shirley's as usual to give a hand, but she kept away from the front first-floor bedroom that was number one guest-room.

The bell rang in the kitchen almost all the time, and Shirley and Roland were kept running.

"I tell you," Shirley admitted, "if we weren't as poor as church mice I'd swear the place was full next time they tried to park her on us."

"How long's she been coming?"

"Two or three times a year for the last—" she thought

for a moment, "—must be about five years, although it seems a life-time. Whew, what a woman!"

Kerry agreed. She was sorry for Shirley, only a nurse would keep a sense of humour with a patient as cantankerous as this.

One morning she could hear Miss Lambert hammering her cane on the floor of her room when the bell wasn't answered quickly enough.

Kerry opened the door and went in smiling. "Goodmorning. Can I get you something?"

The woman, huddled in the armchair by the fire, turned to glare at her.

Miss Lambert felt the cold. She must have, because although the fire was roaring up the chimney and all the windows were closed, she was still so muffled with clothes that only the point of a sharp nose, and two beady eyes, were visible. A shawl was over her head. "Who are you?" she demanded.

"My name's Kerry Mace. What can I get you?"

"You can get me Nurse Trelawney, and when I ring this bell," she reached out her cane to give it another jab, "I expect the nurse to come. That's what I'm paying for. I'm a sick woman." There was nothing wrong with her lungs, Kerry had seldom heard a more piercing voice. "And I need constant medical attention. Get me Nurse Trelawney."

"Very well."

"And, young woman—"

"Yes?" Kerry paused in the doorway.

"Don't come back—I don't like you. I am extremely sensitive to vibrations and yours are alien." She shivered and the great mound of clothing heaved a little. "They are unsympathetic, cold and ugly. I don't want to see you again."

Kerry closed the door quietly. You couldn't be angry

with such an obvious eccentric. The poor old thing was crazy, and if she hadn't been so rich someone might have told her to pull herself together and then perhaps she would have been less objectionable. She might even have felt better.

Shirley was coming panting up the stairs, still drying her hands on a towel. "I was up to my elbows in the pastry bowl. What the dickens does she want now?"

"Medical attention," Kerry mimicked shrilly. "What do you think she pays for, eh? Get up there, Nurse Trelawney, because she doesn't want to see me again. I've got nasty vibrations."

Shirley exploded into laughter and hurried on.

Garth and Tim and Aunt Flora were amused at her tale, too. "That'll teach you," said Tim. "You were told to keep out of her way. Roland says she bites if anybody gets too close."

"And don't think he's joking!" said Kerry. "If she doesn't do that I'll bet she takes a swipe at them with her cane."

But she was sorry for Shirley. Miss Elvira Lambert must be a full-time job and, except for the money, distinctly unrewarding.

That night Kerry and Garth were going out. They had considered a cinema, checking the local newspaper for something they wanted to see and finding nothing interesting decided to do what they often did. Just drive along and make up their minds as they went.

They usually did this at least once a week. There was a standing arrangement now that Wednesdays should be foursomes with Tim and Clare. Mondays and Fridays they usually went out alone unless Miss Drury came for a meal—but she hadn't joined them more than a couple of times. Other evenings were spent doing the farm's clerical work, with Kerry helping; sitting reading, or watching

TV; or walking to the White Bear to meet whoever happened to be there.

It was a pleasant routine. Kerry sometimes felt that it had gone on forever and that it would never change. She couldn't have said if she hoped it would or not.

It had been wash-day and in spite of modern equipment she was a little tired. Seated by Garth in the car, she lay back, relaxing, conscious of the smooth hum of the engine, the pleasure of having him beside her.

He said: "Shall we make for the Dolphin?"

That was a smart roadhouse about twenty miles away which specialised in seafood. Their scampi and lobster were delicious, and Kerry nodded. "Lovely, although I don't know if I'm dressed for it."

She was wearing her grey flannel suit and pink silk blouse and perhaps it would be all right, although folk did tend to put on cocktail dresses for the Dolphin.

"You'll do beautifully," Garth told her, and then, quite casually: "You never wear that stole I gave you."

"No."

"Didn't you like it? We could change it."

There was no sense in lying. She'd only get herself tangled up. "Someone took it that very first night," she said quietly. "Clare and I found it torn to shreds on the beach."

CHAPTER ELEVEN

She daren't look at him. He still drove at the same speed, his eyes on the road ahead. Then, after a long time, he said: "Why didn't you tell me?"

"Your aunt thought it would worry you."

"She knew?"

"She was up when Clare and I came back from the beach."

"You mean the cove?" He didn't wait for her answer. "You're sure it was the stole?"

"It was the stole."

Then silence again, broken by Kerry. "Do you believe in her ghost, Garth? The rest do."

He spoke quietly. "When you're out on the moors at night, or walking by the sea, you feel very small and insignificant, and you realise just how little you do know or understand about life. Even less about death. The most important things to us are hate and love, and how do we know that they finish when we stop breathing? If the hate or the love's big enough it might go on."

Like the way I feel for you, she thought. If I were dying and I knew you loved me, as Miranda did even if you had quarrelled, my last thoughts would be anguish for all I was losing. That would be the pain, the regret, not death itself. With all the strength in my soul I would try to stay. I shouldn't want Heaven, only to stay with you.

Again silence fell between them. She dare not imagine what his thoughts were.

The Dolphin was fairly crowded but a waiter found them a table. They were old customers and he welcomed them by name, promising that the lobster was superb tonight.

A couple of faces were familiar. A man in his early thirties, with bright red hair, and a pretty plump girl, who waved as Kerry and Garth passed and leaned from their table to say: "Hello, how's things?" Roy Jones, 'Ginger' and Brenda, his wife. Ginger was a policeman whom Garth had known since they were boys together. Kerry had met the couple before and liked them. The first time she knew she reminded them of Miranda; but, along with most of Garth's friends, they had come to forget that, and now she was someone in her own right.

The waiter was right. The lobster was superb. They ate their meal with a white wine that had a dry and delicious taste, and Kerry gave herself over to the delight of the moment. That was the only thing to do. Enjoy being with Garth, listening to him. making him smile, and try to forget the shadows that lurked behind them.

They paused for a minute at Roy's table, then went out to the parking lot. The night was cold and Kerry dug in her pocket for her gloves.

"Drat it!" she exclaimed. "I must have left them inside."

"I'll fetch them. Get into the car and keep warm." He gave her the keys and turned back.

She walked slowly across the parking lot. There seemed to be hardly anyone about. The few cars standing there were empty, their owners inside the roadhouse. She saw the three men coming towards her without really noticing them at all, until one stopped, fair and square in front of her. "Evening," he said.

Automatically, she replied: "Good evening."

"All by yourself?"

"No."

"You could have fooled me." The other two laugned, and Kerry thought impatiently: Oh, go away.

She tried to walk past, but one of them caught her arm. Surprised and angered, she said icily: "Don't do that."

"Now, Blondie, don't be standoffish." They weren'ι drunk, but they'd had enough to make them stupid or they would have realised that they'd picked the wrong girl.

She wasn't scared but she was furious. She lashed out with her foot and caught the one who held her a sharp crack on the ankle.

He tightened his hold, his face incredulous. "Why, you

70

little—'' He shook her and his friends crowded closer, their faces ugly.

Frightened, she called out: "Garth!"

He came running. The trio turned and then moved together waiting for him, and he hit one of them so hard that he spun round before he fell. The other two didn't wait, and Garth turned again on the man who was dragging himself to his knees.

"Don't!" Kerry begged. Now she was frightened in earnest. Not for Garth or herself, but frightened of the expression on his face. And so was his victim. He was on his knees. He stayed there, staring up, eyes scared.

"We wouldn't have hurt her," he whimpered. "It was only a bit of fun. For God's sake."

Kerry clung to Garth's arm. "Get away," she told the man. "Get *away!*"

He bolted off like a rabbit into the night.

Ginger and Brenda walked into the parking lot, and seeing the man running, and Kerry holding Garth, Ginger came rushing over. "What's up?"

"Three young toughs thought I was on my own," said Kerry. "Only they weren't so tough, as it happened." Her voice was unsteady. "Garth nearly killed them."

"Good for him," said Ginger. "I could have told them that was a mistake." He grinned at Garth, who smiled back. "You want me to do anything?" Ginger asked.

"Like what?"

"Like chasing them."

"No," said Kerry. "Let them go. They had a lesson."

Ginger was still chuckling. "I'll bet they did. I'd like to have seen it. He's got a black, murderous temper, has this one. We used to get into some beautiful scraps together when we were kids."

The evening ended in their going round to Ginger and Brenda's for coffee and staying well after midnight listen-

71

ing to records. It was an enjoyable rounding off the day.

Driving back Kerry said: "I've had a lovely time."

"Have you? I'm glad. I'm sorry about that business in the parking lot."

"No harm done." She didn't want to think about it. "I didn't know you had a reputation for having a black temper," and put laughter into her words, teasing him.

But his profile was unsmiling, his voice very quiet. "There are a good many things you don't know about me, Kerry."

She wanted to say: "What? Tell me all the things I don't know." But she couldn't. She could do nothing at all but sit still and silent, watching the headlights of the car cut through the dark night.

Miss Lambert had relatives even if she didn't have friends. They came to see her, looking apprehensive before they went in and cowered when they came out.

"She's the one with the money," said Roland cynically. "If she wasn't they wouldn't cross the road for her." He sighed gustily. "Life's very unfair, y'know, Kerry. Old Elvira, one of the most unpleasant people I know, lording it over everybody. And she didn't even earn her cash. Inherited it, that's what she did, the whole darn' firm. Silver spoon from the first. It ought to have choked her."

Kerry kept out of the woman's way. She let the bell ring or the cane thump now, feeling sorry for Shirley but knowing that there was nothing she could do about it. Even when she carried food in, Miss Lambert drew back as though she was likely to catch something.

"I thought I said I didn't want to see you again," she snapped. "It is most important that I should have only sympathetic vibrations around me."

So that was that, and Roland and Shirley had to carry the trays no matter how busy they were.

About the only thing she could do to help was shopping, and when she and Clare planned a Saturday in the nearest town she had a long list from Shirley.

Claire wanted a new cocktail dress and they had a marvellous morning choosing and trying, before they settled on a turquoise number that flattered her slim figure and long legs.

"Tim's going to live it," Kerry said. "I don't know about Aunt Flora, though. Discreet but sexy, I should call it. How's she going to take to that?"

Clare smiled. "It's got a high neck and long sleeves. What's there to worry her?"

They were having coffee after lunch when a girl came towards them. It was Brenda. She had to be told what they'd bought, and stayed chatting. Kerry hadn't seen her since that evening at the Dolphin, a couple of weeks ago, and now Brenda said: "That roughhouse wasn't very nice for you, was it?"

Clare pricked up her ears. "What roughhouse? What have you been up to?"

"There was a bit of an argument in the parking lot. Some characters tried to get fresh with me and Garth sorted them out."

Brenda beamed. "He surely did. My, how they ran!" She gurgled with laughter. "I must fly. You don't know how lucky you are, free and single. Wait till you get yourselves husbands and you won't have so much time for sitting around."

When she had gone, Clare said: "Why didn't you tell us about the trouble in the Dolphin parking lot?"

"It was nothing. It was over in a moment." She hadn't wanted to talk about it, that was why. She didn't now, but she said: "Roy says Garth's always had a black

73

temper. You'd never think it, would you? I've never seen him in a temper before.''

"He was that night?"

"Yes. He knocked the man down who'd been holding me, and the other two ran. Then he turned on the man again." She bit her lip. "I thought he was going to kill him. He looked dangerous. Quiet, and deadly somehow. The man was too scared to move. He just crouched there. It didn't seem like Garth at all.''

Clare said hurriedly: "Most folk have a temper if they're roused. He'd a good reason for being mad, hadn't he? I think I'll buy some hair spray while I'm here. Shall we get the bill?''

"All right.'' Kerry watched her call the waitress and pick up the bill. But her mind was on something else. More pieces of the jigsaw were clicking into place.

"I'm glad I made him take me to the cove,'' she had told Clare. "At least I know all there is to know now."

"Do you?'' Clare had said. And Garth had told her in that strange, flat voice: "There are a good many things you don't know about me, Kerry . . .''

The two girls went out into the busy street.

"Ginger didn't merely say Garth's temper was black.'' Kerry spoke abruptly. "He said it was murderous. He was joking, of course.''

"Of course,'' agreed Clare.

"How bad was the quarrel between Garth and Miranda?''

They walked on, not looking at each other, speaking casually as though this was hardly important at all. "Who's to know?'' said Clare.

"But there was talk?''

"There always is. I've never seen Garth angry since. Some of them think that proves it.''

"Proves what?''

74

Kerry knew the answer, although Clare wouldn't say it. Knew it would be: "Proves he killed Miranda."

CHAPTER TWELVE

It was as though she had always known this, too. The kind of rumours that were whispered and hushed. But even if they believed them, there was more pity than blame for Garth. They knew that he had loved Miranda, they knew that he suffered now.

And there was something else in the last few days. Something to do with the date. Wednesday of the coming week was ringed on the calendar in the kitchen and when she asked: "Is this a birthday?" Miss Drury shook her head.

She didn't offer any information. She went on with her work of cleaning the kitchen stove, and Kerry knew that it had to be something to do with Miranda.

She asked Tim. "It was the day she came," he said.

"Why do you ring it?"

"Aunt Flora does, I suppose."

This wasn't the only house that remembered. In the White Bear that night she overheard Jock say: "Comes round again, doesn't it? Doesn't seem that long."

"What are you expecting?" she asked Clare. Clare was the only person she could talk to freely, perhaps because she was her best friend.

Clare shook her head. "Last year someone swore they saw a boat on the rocks again, and the whole village tore down. There was no sign of a boat, of course, but I think they almost believed that Miranda would be washed ashore, that time would be put back."

"Was Garth there?" Was he ready to wade into the waters again, to swim against the tide to find her?

"No. He was away, and then they said that was why she hadn't come. She was waiting for Garth."

"It's horrible."

"No one will go down to the cove this time. There's a sort of taboo on it now. They all keep away, but they'll still peer through their windows, looking for lights out at sea, and in the morning a few of them will find an excuse to go up to the farm."

Miss Drury cleaned Miranda's room. Kerry knew that she always kept it swept and tidy, presumably when Kerry was out of the house because she had never seen her do it. But this week it was done openly. She brought down the rugs and moved furniture and when Kerry asked if she should help, she was told: "That's all right, my dear, you've plenty to do."

You could pretend that this was ordinary housework. The room had to be kept clean. But you still couldn't get rid of the feeling that it was more like preparation for a guest arriving.

Flora Drury was putting fresh sheets on the bed, and books on the bedside table, and Kerry's flesh crawled each time she looked down the little coridor, through the open door, and saw her.

She told Garth, but he only said: "She's doing no harm."

"But she *is*. To herself. She's making herself believe that Miranda's coming back to that room." There was horror in Kerry's voice.

"She's cleaning it," he said. "It's a pleasant room and we do occasionally have visitors. Maybe she's getting it ready for someone."

"Who?"

He shrugged. "She'll tell us when she's ready." And that was all he would say.

Tim, too, seemed to think Kerry was making a fuss about nothing. A room was being cleaned, that was hardly a world-shaking event.

"It's Miranda's."

"It's still a room and it still has to be cleaned."

She said abruptly: "What do you think will happen on Wednesday night?"

He looked at though he didn't understand, but when she touched the calendar, he didn't have to follow her pointing finger. "Nothing. What could?"

"That's what I'm asking. That's what I want someone to tell me."

But no one did. She spent the Wednesday afternoon at Shirley's and there, too, was an oppressive heaviness. It was a dank day, cold and yet breathless, and when Kerry was through with the work she hardly felt that she had the energy to walk back to the farm.

Shirley was preparing for another two guests.

"They're nice old dears, terribly grateful for anything you do for them. I'll say that for Miss Lambert—she makes you appreciate everyone else."

Kerry walked slowly to the farm. She and Garth were going out with Tim and Clare. It was their usual Wednesday date and tonight there was a comedy film showing. They would probably be late out, so Clare would be staying at the farm, as she often did.

Tea was like most of the other teas had been, a large and satisfying meal. Afterwards Kerry and Miss Drury washed-up and after a while Clare arrived, and Neil.

He'd come to watch a television programme, he said. There was nothing out of the ordinary about that, but Kerry wondered if he had come tonight because Garth and Tim didn't want to leave Aunt Flora alone. No one was admitting it. They were sticking firmly to routine, but Neil was here, stolid and reliable, carrying a bucket of coal into the drawing-room to stoke up for the evening. He was staying the night, too, but that wasn't unusual, either. There were more than enough rooms.

The film was funny. They enjoyed it, and Kerry, glancing at Clare's smiling face, at Garth and Tim, tall and broad-shouldered and strong, wondered if she was the only one who had a sick feeling in her stomach, who was dreading the night.

Back at the farm, they all had hot drinks, and chatted about nothing in particular. Afterwards, they said goodnights all round and Kerry went to her room.

She wasn't tired now. Perhaps the relaxing evening had refreshed her, or perhaps it was because her nerves were so tense that she knew she hadn't a chance of sleep.

She didn't even undress. She sat by her window, listening to the sea. As Miss Drury had said on the first morning, sometimes it seemed to come nearer till you could almost believe it was all round the house.

It was very near tonight, but whispering softly. Not like the night, two years ago, when Miranda came. There had been a storm then. If there had been a storm tonight Kerry didn't believe she would be able to sit here alone.

She wasn't enjoying it much, anyway. She was shivering so much that she put on a coat, but that only helped a little and at last she stood up.

She would go downstairs and get a book, or something. She couldn't just sit here all night.

The house was dark and still, no sound anywhere except for the boards creaking beneath her feet, and the grandfather clock ticking in the hall. She opened the drawing-room door. This fire should still be glowing embers. The kitchen stove was damped down for the night, there was no comfort there.

She knelt on the sheepskin rug and held out her hands and she was still there when she heard the footsteps in the hall. They were firm and quick, and they were Garth's, she would recognise them anywhere.

She had been waiting for this. She hadn't really wanted a book. That was why she hadn't switched on the light, sitting here in the dark. If Garth went out tonight she had to go too.

She heard the kitchen door click before she followed him. He could have only one destination, so that even if she missed him she would find him at the cove. But as she slipped out of the farmhouse she saw his tall figure ahead, a grey shadow against the greyer night.

He didn't look back once, and he walked so quickly that she had to break into a stumbling run. He was hurrying as though he might be late, as though every minute mattered. If he had been going to meet his living love he couldn't have gone more eagerly, and tears ran down Kerry's face so that she had to blink or she would have lost sight of him.

If she hadn't been here before with Clare she would have had difficulty in finding the track. It still wasn't easy, because that had been in daylight and tonight there was shifting mist, rising like fog from the sea. Several times loose stones slipped beneath her feet and she had to choke back a cry. She could still see Garth. He was almost on the beach now.

Last year someone said they had seen a ship. Suppose when the mist parted she saw a shape out there, patterned with the lights of windows, tilted at a crazy angle? And suppose Garth plunged into the sea and swam out towards it?

She called his name and saw him whirl around.

"Garth, it's Kerry." She reached him and clutched his coat. "Don't stay, Garth, let's go back."

"Kerry, what the devil are you doing here?"

"I followed you."

"Why?"

"I couldn't let you go to her. You came because you thought she might be here, didn't you?"

He brushed a hand across his forehead. "I don't know. I came because I knew I should get no rest. Because I thought if I stayed on this beach tonight I might convince myself that it's all superstition. If she's haunting anyone, it's me. I murdered her."

"It was an accident."

"Yes, it was an accident. But whether she jumped off that cliff, or whether she was thrown over, it was because of me."

"Thrown over?"

"Don't tell me you haven't considered that. Not since you hung on to my arm to stop me from half-killing that man in the car parking lot. You haven't forgotten what Roy said? He went to school with me, but he doesn't know me as well as the people round here. Nor did he know Miranda like they did. It's an accident in his books. She went too near the edge and she slipped. But I know that wasn't the way she died." His voice broke.

"Did you throw her over?" The mist was all around them. She could feel it like cold trailing fingers on her face. She stood close to Garth, but it seemed to hide him from her.

"I could have. Roy's right about my temper. It's always been black and murderous. It used to frighten me as a child; it was like someone else taking possession of me. I learnt to control it as I grew older, but that night—I honestly don't know. I was angry enough to kill her. I could have done it."

He looked down at his hands and Kerry took them both in hers. "No," she said. "You might hit a man, you

80

might half kill him, but you couldn't pick up a girl and throw her down on to those rocks.''

"How do you know?''

"I just know.'' She looked into his face, his eyes. There was agony in them but none of the blind cruelty that would smash a thing as lovely as Miranda.

She put her arms around him, drawing him close, and he held her tight. She could feel his body shaking.

"Thank God for you,'' he said huskily. "Oh, Kerry, thank God for you.''

CHAPTER THIRTEEN

Come back to the farm,'' Kerry tried to persuade him.

"Not yet,'' he said. "But *you* must go.''

"Not alone.''

"Please, Kerry. This is no place for you.''

"I'm staying,'' she insisted.

The night went slowly. Sometimes the bay was almost clear, so that the moon shone on the water and the rocks and the shadows of the boulders. A moment later the mist rolled up, blanketing it all, then merged into wisps that moved and swirled like dancers.

It was very cold even with Garth's arm around her, but she would have stayed if the sea had frozen over. Nothing could have made her leave Garth there alone.

At four-thirty he looked at his watch and said: "We'll go.''

Was it past the time when Miranda came? Kerry didn't ask. She just turned gratefully for the track up from the cove. Garth's hand guided and helped her and when they reached the top she looked down again.

"Have we proved anything?" she said.

He shook his head.

"Your aunt thinks she'll come."

"My aunt thinks she never went away."

"Do you want her to come?"

He said slowly: "I'd give half the years I have left to have the weight of her death off me, but no, I don't want her back." And then, without any warning at all: "Will you marry me, Kerry?"

She swayed against the wind. "What did you say?"

"You must care for me or you wouldn't have stayed here and you wouldn't have come to the cove tonight. And I love you, Kerry."

"You never said that before."

"I shouldn't be saying it now. I've told myself a hundred times that I've no right to involve you. There's something hellish here and I don't want it to touch you. I should send you away from Polbryn. Would you go?"

"If you did."

"I can't leave. We've farmed this land for hundreds of years. It's the only place I could make my home."

She understood that. There was something wild and free about this coastline. She could believe that a man, born and reared here, would never be happy anywhere else. She felt its spell herself, and knew that for all the terror, she loved it, too.

He said: "If you say no, I'll understand."

"I won't say no."

He held her gently, kissed her gently, and promised: "I'll keep you safe. Nothing shall harm you, I swear."

"I know I shall be safe now," she said.

It was only in her imagination that the wisps of mist had become colder and more menacing, moving like figures across their path. This was a wrecker cove. "More

82

men and women have died there than anyone will ever know," Flora Drury had told Kerry. "We've lived with ghosts for generations."

She clutched Garth's hand. "Let's go home," she whispered, and they hurried through the mist, over the rough grasses and shingle, back to the farmhouse.

There were lights. In the kitchen Miss Drury sat in her usual armchair. Tim and Neil were there, and Clare's face was deathly pale against her dark red housecoat.

As Garth and Kerry walked in, Clare said in a strangled voice: "Where were you?"

Garth answered with a question. "What happened here?"

"You went to the cove!" That was his aunt. "You need not have done that because Miranda was here. She tapped on our doors. You remember how she used to do that?" Garth nodded. "So we got up and came downstairs."

Kerry could hardly breathe. Clare looked terrified, Tim had his arm around her, and there was perspiration on Neil's forehead.

When Garth spoke, his voice seemed as loud as though he were shouting. "Kerry and I are getting married."

"What?" His aunt stiffened. No one else said a word but they looked as though they had heard something impossible.

"We decided just now." Garth held Kerry's hand and smiled at her, and she wished she could believe it herself instead of feeling that it was all part of a charade.

"You *can't*." That was his aunt, looking old and frightened. "You know that, Garth."

He turned to Tim and Clare and Neil. "Aren't you going to congratulate us?"

"Of course we do." Clare's eyes looked as they had done when she found the stole. "I—I only hope—" She faltered and waited for Tim, and Tim said:

"I only hope you realise what you're doing."

"I think so," said Garth.

No one pretended to be glad. Not even when they had decided that it was too late to go back to bed, and made coffee and drank a little of it. Even when the colour was creeping back into Clare's cheeks, and the two girls had gone upstairs, she could only say: "Oh Kerry, I'm so frightened for you."

"What happened tonight? What did Aunt Flora mean, Miranda tapped on your doors?"

"She had a special tap, a sort of little rhythm. She used to do it in the mornings if anyone overslept, and I heard it on my door just after half past four."

"We left the cove at half past four."

Clare said absently: "That was the time of the wreck. Tim has told me that when they carried her into the farm the clock was striking the half hour. I heard it tonight just before the tapping."

"You could have imagined it."

"We could have. I suppose we were all waiting for something." But she didn't mean that. Abruptly she said: "Move into this room, Kerry. It's farther from hers."

"You sound as if you think I'm in danger."

"Miranda was possessive. Even about ordinary things like her clothes and her make-up. No one dared look at Garth while she was around or she'd sulk like a schoolgirl. She even accused me once of preferring him to Tim because we'd talked about an article in a newspaper.

"I'm scared for you." An idea came to her suddenly. "Why don't you come and stay with me? My mother wouldn't mind."

Clare's mother was an older Clare, a gracious woman with a wide circle of friends and a warm welcome for everyone. But Kerry had no intention of moving in on them in their flat, which was ample for two but not for three.

She said almost defiantly: "Thank you, but I'll stay here. Besides if a ghost's after me, it won't make any difference where I am, will it?"

"Don't joke about it." Clare sounded near to hysterics, and Kerry said quietly:

"I'm not. It just sounds like that. I often sound flippant when I'm scared. Perhaps she is here. I'm not sure anymore, but I'll fight her for Garth wherever she is."

Clare picked up a lipstick and touched lips that were still a little unsteady. "You may have to," she said.

By breakfast-time, the neighbours were beginning to drop in. They came to bring things or to borrow things, but really to see and to hear.

Kerry felt that if Miss Drury had met them a finger on her lips saying: "Don't talk too loudly, Miranda's asleep," they would have dropped their voices to a whisper. They honestly had thought she might come back from the sea.

When Beth Lovelace said sympathetically: "You won't have had much rest last night, I'm thinking." Miss Drury nodded. "Not that any of us had much. You couldn't help lying awake remembering," said Beth.

Garth and Tim and Neil hurried to get away. Clare left, too, as soon as breakfast was over, although she might as well have missed it for the amount she ate.

No one ate, or even pretended to, and when Garth kissed Kerry goodbye he put a finger under her chin and tilted it gently. "Take no notice of them," he said.

He left her in the courtyard and it was cold, and she knew that the day ahead was going to be grim.

Garth had asked her to marry him. That should have been enough to send her crazy with happiness, and it was,

85

but she did wish that someone would hear the news without that sick look of shock in their eyes. Even Clare had looked more as though she was hearing something tragic than news of a marriage.

None of the neighbours had been told. They had come and gone and no one had mentioned it. But when they did hear, Kerry knew that their reaction would be the same as Clare's.

She went back into the house now. Beth was leaving and Miss Drury was gathering up the breakfast things. She said: "You and I must have a talk, Kerry."

It had to be about Garth, and Kerry was almost sure she knew what was going to be said.

"Were you serious, about marrying him?" Aunt Flora asked.

"Of course."

"He doesn't love you, you know." Kerry hadn't expected it to be so brutal. "He just hopes you'll help him forget Miranda."

"Perhaps I will."

"Not a love as great as that." Pain grew inside Kerry. "It had to be a great love," Flora Drury said softly, "to keep her here. When she was alive, I knew she loved him, but it's only since she died that I've realised how much.

"I was in love once, I was younger than you, just seventeen and he was nineteen and a fisherman. He was drowned and, like Garth, I wouldn't believe it. I used to wait for him and think he'd come back, and sometimes I was sure I could feel him in the room with me." She smiled, not at Kerry, a sweet and secret smile. "Sometimes I still do.

"But Miranda must have loved Garth more even than my Danny loved me, because she *is* here. The whole village knows it. You can't take him away from her, Kerry."

86

"I love him."

"Yes, I believe it." Aunt Flora stood with the little stack of cups and saucers in her hands. "But I don't think Miranda will give him up, and sometimes she had a very cruel streak."

She said no more. She turned to the sink and began to wash the cups and after a moment or two Kerry got on with her own work.

She didn't go into her bedroom until halfway through the morning, and then she saw the photograph.

It was one of herself and Garth at the party, not the one with the stole, quite a harmless one. Neil had given it to her, and she had stuck it to the mirror on top of the chest of drawers.

Now it lay flat, and both eyes had been gouged through and through so that the face was that of a girl disfigured and blind.

CHAPTER FOURTEEN

Waves of nausea swept over her and she clutched the edge of the chest of drawers. She was more than frightened. This was a warped and evil thing. Whoever, whatever, had done this, was mad.

She tore up the photograph as though that would wipe out the memory, but in the mirror she could still see her own face, and remember the gouged-out eyes . . .

She hurried from the room, shutting the door tightly behind her. When she got downstairs Lissy was in the kitchen. "Is it a fact, then? Are you going to marry Garth?"

Miss Drury sat by impassively. She must have told Lissy she knew nothing about it.

Kerry nodded. "Yes."

Lissy whistled. "They wouldn't believe it at the White Bear. Denis Rawley came in and said Neil had told him, and everybody said he was having us on, so I said I'd come and ask you."

"And now you have," said Kerry.

"Well, congratulations." Lissy made them sound hearty. "You're the dark one, none of us guessed."

Yet she and Garth had been inseparable for weeks. They had been seen together by the White Bear's patrons again and again. Any other girl and man would have been an accepted twosome by now. They were surprised because they still thought of Garth as Miranda's. It had never occurred to them that he would fall in love again.

"When's the wedding going to be?" Lissy wanted to know.

They hadn't had time to talk about that. "I don't really know. Soon, I should think. After all there doesn't seem much point in waiting."

"No, I suppose not." Lissy looked as though she was listening to something else. "I'd better be getting along, I only dashed over for a few minutes."

When Kerry went along to Shirley's, she said what Tim had said. "I hope you realise what you're doing."

"Why shouldn't I?"

"You know that, love."

It was only when she was alone with Garth that Kerry could pretend everything was wonderful. He took her to buy a ring and she sat dazzled in front of trays of glittering stones, trying them on, holding her hand out for Garth to see.

One square-cut emerald caught her eye. It looked frighteningly expensive but Garth had insisted she was to have whatever she wanted and she picked it up. Shen the light caught it, it turned to green fire, and she gasped:

"Isn't this gorgeous?"

The jeweller agreed enthusiastically. He leaned over, pointing out its beauties, how exquisitely it was cut, how the setting had been deisgned by a master.

Garth said: "I like the diamond cluster better."

Until she had seen the emerald, that had been Kerry's choice—a star of diamonds. It was still on her finger while she was handling the emerald. If Garth liked it best, well—perhaps she did too.

She said: "Yes, I think you're right. The diamonds, please." So long as it was Garth's ring, she didn't care what it was like. So long as she knew it was no dream, that she really was going to be his wife.

Everyone wanted to see the ring. They knew that Kerry and Garth had gone to get it, and Clare and Lissy and Shirley were waiting for her to come back.

As the car drew into the courtyard they came running across. "Did you get it? Let's see," Clare was demanding.

Kerry struggled with her glove, careful to lift it over the setting.

"When Tim and Neil see this," Lissy giggled, "they might begin to realise what's expected of them." She gasped. "Oh, that's lovely. Oh, isn't that a beauty!"

Kerry walked into the house with the three girls around her, all admiring and envying. Even Aunt Flora was waiting to see what they had chosen and to declare it was one of the nicest rings she had ever seen.

For a moment there seemed no shadows at all. They were as thrilled at her ring as Miriam and the girls in town would have been.

She said: "They were all beautiful but we liked this best, didn't we, Garth? Although I wasn't sure about an emerald."

She began to tell them about it. "A square one, with a rather modern setting." Suddenly she noticed the silence.

She looked up at Clare, who smiled brightly, then across at Miss Drury. And she knew that Miranda's ring had been an emerald. No one had to tell her. That was why Garth hadn't wanted her to have that ring.

She touched her diamond gently, glad she had chosen it, and thought: I shall never take it off—if I do, the same thing may happen to it, that happened to my stole. I shall wear it always and then no one can steal it from me.

Letters arrived thick and fast as soon as she wrote to her friends. Miriam had sounded slightly grumpy. If Kerry was going to marry her farmer, Miriam supposed she'd have to find someone else to share the apartment.

She hoped Kerry would be happy, although it sounded a bit dull down there and that great big farmhouse would mean an awful lot of work.

Kerry's letter hadn't told them much. She had written about her life, the people she met, but she had said nothing about Miranda. Neither to Miriam not to Aunt Eleanor. If she'd put that on paper they'd have thought she was going out of her mind.

Aunt Eleanor and Uncle Bill's enthusiasm was restrained. They were delighted, of course, that Kerry should be engaged to someone she loved, but they only hoped she had given herself enough time to be sure, and they wished they could have met him and that Australia wasn't so far away.

Their regret was gentle but genuine. If they had known the rest of the story they would have been on the first plane, determined to take her away by force. If Aunt Eleanor had seen that gouged photograph, or the stole torn to shreds; or Garth looking at his hands as though they were a stranger's and saying: "I could have done it, I could have killed her," they wouldn't have wasted time writing letters.

But they didn't know, and Kerry's love cast aside dark

90

shadows, and her ring was a charm against the past.

She had to take it off, of course. You can't do housework and cooking in a diamond ring. But when it had come off she slipped in into its box and put that in her pocket. She was never parted from it.

Until she left it behind at Shirley's. She had been washing her hands and put it on the window ledge of the bathroom. She remembered before she got home and ran all the way back, angry with herself for her carelessness but not really worried.

The door was open and she hurried in. The Corw's Nest was on three floors, the kitchens below in the basement and the bedrooms above the ground floor. Shirley would be in the basement, the bathroom where Kerry had left her ring was upstairs and Kerry rushed for it. She was so glad to see her ring she stood for a moment beaming at it and getting her breath back.

When the phone shrilled out she expected Shirley to answer it. There was an extension on this floor, for the benefit of the guests. The call was probably for Miss Lambert.

Kerry heard her door open and kept out of sight. She didn't want to cause any more touble with the wrong vibrations. Through the crack of the bathroom door she saw Miss Lambert hurrying to answer the phone. Without her mound of blankets and shawls she looked a completely different person, slim and straight. She didn't even look old, and Kerry would never have recognised her voice. When she picked up the phone it was clear and incisive.

She wasn't speaking English and there wasn't enough of it for anyone who didn't speak the language to decide what it might be. Just a few words, brief, authoritative. Then she put down the phone and went back to her room.

The old fraud, thought Kerry. She's got Shirley climbing these stairs a dozen times a day, waiting on her hand and foot, and she's as able to get around as I am. I'd love to walk in now and tell her she's an old hypocrite.

But of course she couldn't. She could only go downstairs, where Shirley was sitting at tea with Roland and say: "Our Elvira is a phony."

"What?" They gaped at her. "What are you doing here?"

"I came back for my ring, I left it in the bathroom. You didn't mind me dashing in?"

"Of course not. Have a cup of tea." Shirley was reaching into a cupboard but Kerry stopped her.

"I must get home. Only there was a phone call while I was upstairs and dear Elvira came out of her room, blithe as a spring lamb, and snapped into it like a company sergeant major."

Roland grinned. "Did you let her know you'd seen her?"

"No. I kept out of sight in the bathroom."

"Pity really. I'd like her to know we're wise to her."

"Did you guess?" Kerry asked.

"Well, I know she's a hypochondriac," said Shirley. "A genuine one. She believes she's ill and most of the time she really feels ill. She put this call through earlier in the day. It has to do with the export firm she owns, and the only thing that could make her forget herself is money. The call meant cash."

The bell rang shrilly and Roland sighed. "Back in character," he said. "All right my goose-that-lays-the-golden-eggs, I'm coming; but if ever we win the lottery, you're going to hear some home truths about yourself."

The last few days had been uneventful. They had been ordinary, normal days with no sounds that couldn't be explained, and they should have made Kerry feel easier.

92

Miranda's door was still open whenever one looked at it, but Kerry had decided it was a faulty lock, although it seemed all right when you turned the knob. Miss Drury said no more, and Clare was obviously trying to make up for her first lack of enthusiasm about Kerry's engagement.

She told Kerry they must have a celebration, just the four of them. Aunt Flóra wouldn't come.

All so normal—yet it was frightening.

Each time Kerry walked upstairs she still had the feeling of being watched. A malignant feeling was in the air, as though someone who hated you bided their time.

There were little things. The cotton reel on the stairs, so that she could have pitched head first on to the tiled floor of the hall. A gas tap on her bedroom fire turned on a little, leaking slowly and insidiously. She smelled it as soon as she walked into the room, but what if it had been during the night and she had been asleep? Of course she might have knocked it on herself, perhaps when she was cleaning, but she could have sworn she hadn't.

Half the things she didn't mention. She was afraid they'd think she was imagining them. Besides, she didn't want Miss Drury to build them up.

But the night she seemed to be starting a heavy cold something happened that she couldn't hide, because she screamed and they all came running.

It had rained heavily and she had got soaked collecting a knitting pattern for Miss Drury. The rain came suddenly and when she got back, her feet squelched like something in a bog and her clothes were sticking to her skin.

Miss Drury was conscience-stricken, insisted on her taking a hot bath, and gave her a stiff whisky.

Protests did no good at all. Kerry tried to beg off the whisky by saying she felt fine, and then spoiled it by sneezing. So the whisky was drunk, an extra hot water bottle was put in the bed and so was Kerry.

She slept heavily, and woke suffocating. For a moment it was a nightmare. She couldn't breathe or see. Something soft as feathers or sea surf was covering her face.

She jerked up in bed, snatching the pillow away. She gulped for breath and screamed and screamed.

Garth reached her first. The terror in her face was reflected in his. He held her close and she sobbed against him as Tim and Miss Drury asked, "What's happened? What's the matter?"

"There was a pillow over my face."

"You mean someone tried to suffocate you?" Garth demanded.

"No." She couldn't honestly say that. "It was just on my face." But it had been as horrible as though there was force behind it. She could still feel the yielding softness.

Garth was saying gently: "You're a little light-headed darling, you tossed about and buried your face into the pillow and it gave you a nightmare."

Miss Drury picked it up from where it had fallen. She held it to her face and then she said: "It's damp—damp and salt with sea water."

CHAPTER FIFTEEN

Quickly taking it from her, Garth said: "The window's open. It's rain." His voice brooked no contradiction, but his aunt said:

"You must move from your room, Kerry. Come into

the one next to mine. There's a connecting door." She put a hand on Kerry's forehead. "We don't want this cold turning into a fever. You need someone within call."

"I'd like to do that." Next to Miss Drury, both Garth's and Tim's rooms would be between her and Miranda's.

She felt hot and more than a little feverish, but very sure that she couldn't sleep here. Garth looked as though he might be going to object and she reached out to grab her dressing-gown. "Let's go, please."

The room was aired. It was the one they had been using as a guest room and until now, the connecting door had been bolted. Now Miss Drury pushed it open. "I'll leave the lamp on by your bed, and if you want anything at all call me."

"I'll sleep," Kerry promised.

Garth looked in at her from the doorway. "And no more nightmares, darling."

Next morning she felt a little ashamed of herself, because that was what it must have been, just as everything else had been an accident, a coincidence. She was letting her imagination play tricks on her.

The cold was much better, Miss Drury's treatment had been effective, and Kerry insisted on getting up.

Garth wasn't pleased about that. When he saw her, there was quite an argument about whether she should go back and have a least a day in bed. But she stood her ground and Miss Drury promised that she shouldn't set foot outside, or do anything that was likely to harm her.

"All right," he agreed grudgingly, "but look after her because she's very precious to me."

"I know," said his aunt. "I'll take care of her."

Kerry had a struggle to get any work done, because Miss Drury was taking her promise seriously. She kept as close to Kerry as a shadow. Most of the time she made her stay in the kitchen, polishing the ornate silver that was rarely used now but taken out of its cupboard every couple of months or so for cleaning.

"You need an even temperature until that cold's quite gone," she said. "It was my fault you caught it, sending you for that pattern."

"Nonsense," said Kerry. "How could you know it was going to rain like that? Anyhow I'm all right now."

"All the same, you must take it easy."

Kerry moved towards the door and she called quite shrilly: "Where are you going?"

"To my room, for some tissues."

"I'll fetch them."

"Of course you won't. You're not running up and down stairs for me. I'll get them myself."

"Kerry, please," Miss Drury pleaded, "let me get them."

"Because I've a cold?"

"Not entirely, you know that." Kerry had suspected it. "There was sea water on that pillow last night."

"It was rain," Kerry protested.

"She isn't going to let you marry Garth."

"She can't stop me!" She touched her ring, her talisman for happiness. "We will marry. Please believe that. Help us and try to be happy for us."

"I try to help you. I always have, but she isn't letting him go and she must hate you very much."

Garth looked in during the morning. "How's the invalid?"

"Fine."

"You're still flushed. I'm not sure that our climate suits you. When we're married, would you like to move away from here?"

She'd go anywhere he wanted to go but this was his land and his life. She mustn't let him be afraid for her and she mustn't let her own nerves play silly tricks.

"When we're married?" she said. "When are we going to be married?"

"Whenever you say."

"Soon? As soon as we can."

"Then the end of next month?"

They fixed the date. "Do you think anyone will come to it?" She spoke thoughtfully.

"Of course they will! They'll be clamouring for invitations, and if you don't have Clare for a bridesmaid we'll have trouble with Tim."

They told his aunt first. She said: "I wish you happiness." She kissed Kerry and held out a hand to draw Garth towards her, but there was still fear in her eyes, her face was haggard with it.

Later on, she suggested that they might like her to find somewhere else to live, that they would prefer the farm to themselves. Kerry was quite horrified at the idea. Norbrook Farm must remain home for them all, just as it had always done.

The following days were busy. There was so much to be done, everyone accepted their invitations.

Garth had suggested holding the reception at the White Bear, but Miss Drury said no. A Drury was always married from Norbrook, certainly the head of the family had to be. Besides, the White Bear was a small pub and Norbrook was a large house, much better for a reception. She sat with lists of names, planning where the guests would sit and what they would eat.

There was suddenly a near-delirious air of anticipation. Clare was to be the only bridesmaid, Kerry had no closer friend in Polbryn. She and Clare chose the material for their dresses and Trix, who was married to a fisherman, made them.

Although she was country born and bred, Trix could

have made a living as a high-class dressmaker. She loved the feel of fabrics and handled them like an artist. She had Clare and Kerry draped in yards of shimmering brocade while she stitched and pinned, pulled and straightened.

She smiled up at Kerry, mumbling a little because she was holding pins between her lips.

"You'll be a lovely bride."

"Thank you."

Trix smoothed the skirt. "I hope this dress will be luckier than the last."

Miranda's. The dress upstairs that had never been worn. Trix wasn't a tactless person, she wouldn't say a thing like that unthinkingly. In her way she was warning Kerry, and Kerry could only say: "It will be."

Presents began to arrive. As Norbrook Farm was fully furnished and equipped, it wasn't easy to choose gifts but the sentiments were genuine even if some of the wedding presents were duplicated.

Kerry still went down to help Shirley, who was busier than ever. There was another couple of guests now—two brothers, elderly, extremely courteous in direct contrast with Miss Lambert. Roland called them Bill and Ben the Flowerpot Men, because their surname was Potts and they were fresh air fanatics. Windows thrown wide open, cold baths every morning.

Kerry saw very little of them, although one of them became a brain teaser for odd moments. He had a vaguely familiar face She couldn't place him at all but he was like someone, perhaps an actor she'd seen on television. It niggled irritatingly in the back of her mind, the way a resemblance can.

Shirley said she couldn't think of anyone who looked like Mr. Potts, except perhaps his brother, but then it wasn't an unusual face. A little florid, a little fleshy, pleasant—especially after Miss Lambert. He and his brother had been estate agents, they owned blocks of property in various parts of the country. You could find a Mr. Potts in most towns.

Kerry agreed, and stopped wondering who he reminded her of.

The days seemed to be going slowly now, there were still two whole weeks to the wedding, and she was impatient for it to come. Not only because she loved Garth but because of the little doubts. He loved her, he told her often now, but he never said that he hadn't loved Miranda more. And he hadn't been able to bear the thought of an emerald engagement ring. Kerry wouldn't have been human not to remember what his aunt had said. "He's only marrying you to try to forget her."

There was still that undercurrent of menace in the house. Miss Drury wouldn't let her go anywhere alone if she could help it, especially upstairs. She made no secret of her fear that Kerry was in danger, and although Garth and Tim and Clare never admitted as much they watched her too.

She tried to laugh about it, but she didn't really feel like laughter. Especially at night, even though the door to Miss Drury's room was ajar. She heard footsteps more than once, not Tim's or Garth's. They were too light.

Once she got out of bed and crossed to the door and heard Miss Drury call: "Kerry."

"Yes?"

"Don't go out." The older woman was out of bed too, gripping Kerry's wrist with surprising strength.

"I heard someone," Kerry said.

"I often hear her. *Don't go out*."

Anyhow the footsteps had died away. The house was still. She might have imagined she had heard them, if Aunt Flora had not been so pale in the moonlight.

CHAPTER SIXTEEN

The showdown with Elvira Lambert had to come. Kerry was sorry, because it did seem like letting Shirley down.

It all began quite simply. Miss Lambert was having her bath and Kerry, passing the open bedroom door, went in to collect the breakfast tray.

She took it downstairs, washed up and put the things away. Most of Shirley's time went in cooking because special diets were part of the service. Roland did the heavy work about the house, and Kerry managed as much cleaning as she could. She was back upstairs, making beds when she heard the bell ring and Miss Lambert calling at the top of her voice.

It sounded so urgent that Kerry ran. The woman was in the middle of her bedroom, cane tip on the bell, eyes fairly glittering with rage. Shirley came, too, so did Roland. Even the flowerpot men opened their door.

When a complete audience was there, Miss Lambert took her cane off the bell-push and jabbed it at Kerry. "She's been in here again!"

"How do you know?" Roland demanded.

She waved her cane around her. "The vibrations. They've been disturbed. She's left them sharp and savage. Can't you feel it?" Roland said he couldn't. Shirley murmured something soothing, but Miss Lambert was having none of it. "Either that girl leaves the house at once or I go."

Shirley opened her mouth to speak but Miss Lambert stopped her.

"I mean it." She sounded so spiteful that Kerry had no doubt at all.

She said: "I just picked up your tray, but if it worries you I'm prepared to give you my word I won't do it again. I'll never come near your room."

Miss Lambert stood, grotesque in her dressing-gown and layered shawls, eyes closed, lips clamped together, shaking her head. "Out of the house! Her or me!"

Shirley took her arm and managed to get her into a chair. She signalled the rest with her eyes and Roland and Kerry moved out. The Potts closed their door.

Downstairs Kerry said: "I can't tell you how sorry I am about that. I picked up the tray and brought it down but I can't imagine how she knew."

"Guessed probably, the old baggage," said Roland. "Or heard you. The bathroom's near the top of the stairs, she'd know no one came up, she'd hear you go down and if her tray had gone she'd know you'd taken it."

"I might be able to keep out of her sight but I can't be sure. Will she simmer down?"

He grimaced. "If Shirley can't quiet her, no one can. Little wonder her relatives are so grateful to us. I suppose it's worse for them. She's only a business proposition to us, but she's their kith and kin. Imagine that!"

Kerry grinned. "I'd rather not."

They waited for Shirley. Shirley was quite a time and when she came she wasn't smiling. She looked angry, flopped into a chair and said: "There ought to be a law against women like her. She's mental. No, she isn't, if she were I'd feel sorry for her. She's just selfish and stupid and no one has ever said 'No' to her in the whole of her life."

"I gather she didn't see reason," said Roland.

"Reason! What's that? She wouldn't know reason if it

upped and bit her. Oh no, she can't have Kerry under the same roof. It's Kerry or Miss Lambert and wouldn't I just love to tell her what to do."

"But you can't," said Kerry. She knew how much Miss Lambert was paying and it was the best part of Shirley and Roland's bank account. "As a matter of fact I was going to ask you if you could get along without me. I do have my hands rather full with the wedding so near."

"You've been a darling," said Shirley gratefully. "I don't know what I should have done without you. I've been a selfish beast to let you come when I know how busy you are. There must be a bit of Elvira in me, too!"

Kerry laughed. They had a farewell drink, toasted the downfall of Miss Lambert, and let her bell ring for minutes before Roland went up to answer it.

Kerry went back to the farm and told them she had been sacked. Aunt Flora was indignant, both for Shirley and for Kerry, but the others turned it into a joke, and considering he had never set eyes on Miss Lambert, Tim did a very passible imitation of her waving her stick at Kerry and accusing her of sabotaging the vibrations.

Shirley cycled up that evening to apologise all over again, as though it had been her fault, and although Kerry tried to cheer her up she was still miserable about it.

"I would have been leaving in any case," Kerry consoled her.

"Tell her that," urged Tim. "Tell her Kerry's getting married and perhaps she'll send her a present. A spare vibration or something."

Kerry shuddered. "I wouldn't dare to open it."

"Anyhow," Shirley consoled herself, "she always does go home again. It can't be for more than another few weeks. Oh dear, I'm going to miss you, Kerry, and it isn't only because of the work."

She cycled away, still looking glum.

Trix had the dresses ready days before they were needed. She had made a beautiful job of them. The two girls had a mannequin parade in the drawing-room of the farm and all the women came to say how gorgeous they were, and how clever Trix was with her fingers.

Kerry's dress still needed the slightest of adjustments. To her it looked quite perfect but Trix thought one shoulder drooped the faintest degree—a stitch here and a stitch there should fix it.

"I'll do it tomorrow," she promised.

The next day she came and Clare ran upstairs to fetch the dress. They were in the kitchen, the men hadn't quite finished their tea. Kerry went into the drawing-room and slipped out of her blouse and skirt while Trix took out her rolls of pins and her box of silks.

And then Clare came back. She was as white as chalk. "It's gone!" she cried.

"Not my dress?" Kerry whispered.

"Come and see." Clare grabbed her arm and with Trix behind them they ran up the stairs. The dress had been laid across an armchair. There was no sign of it—but there was still a dress there.

Trix recognised it. She stared and her eyes grew huge. "Miranda's!" she whispered.

This dress looked as fresh as new. As it should do, for it had never been worn. Miranda should have worn it to marry Garth, and now it was here as though she was still to be his bride.

"No," said Kerry. *"No!"* She was screaming and didn't care. She heard the others coming, the questions asked, and she pointed to Miranda's dress. "Someone's taken my dress and left this. Who did it? Who *did* it?"

"Come away," said Aunt Flora. She put an arm around the girl. "We'll find your dress."

"Like my stole?"

She knew she was hysterical. These last days had been hard on her, always waiting for something horrible to happen. She suddenly broke from the older woman's hands and ran into the corridor. "Can you hear me? Are you there, Miranda?" she shouted. "I want my wedding dress back! Give it back to me!"

Garth caught her, holding her, shaking her a little. "Hush, darling, don't tear yourself to pieces like this." He led her away, back downstairs, poured out some brandy and made her swallow it.

She was still half-wild with distress and terror. That other dress lying there had been almost like seeing Miranda, as though no matter what happened she would always be there. Near enough to whisper to Garth in the night, to call him from Kerry's side.

There were no roses now but the perfume of them came from the bowl of *pot pourri* on Miranda's writing-desk in the window. Kerry got up and crossed to the desk. "Take this stuff away. Every time I smell it I see yellow roses. It's either roses or that perfume."

Clare took the bowl and slipped from the room with it, and Kerry said: "All these things that belonged to her or that she chose—that picture and this desk—I want them to go. I know they're beautiful but they mean that the house is full of her."

Garth said quietly: "All right, they shall go."

She didn't fell triumph. She didn't feel anything. She didn't even think this was going to work because Miranda wasn't that desk or a picture on the wall; she was a feeling, a rustle of a skirt, a sound in the night, a breath of perfume.

But Neil and Garth and Tim moved the writing-desk into one of the outhouses. There was a faint pattern left on the wallpaper where the picture had been, and the

104

room looked less attractive. Kerry knew it, so did everyone else.

Then she said: "Her bedroom."

"You don't want it emptied tonight?" protested Tim.

"It's like a shrine," Kerry said bleakly. "It's still hers. We'll imagine her here as long as it's like that."

"What do you want to do with it?" asked Miss Drury.

"I want it changed, made to look like the other rooms."

"No." Aunt Flora's lips were working. "The things she left down here, put those away if you like. But leave her room. It would be like killing her again."

Kerry saw Garth flinch. "Very well," he said. "Lock the room and leave it."

She didn't argue. She knew that his aunt's words had cut deep into his heart.

Trix left soon afterwards. She said: "I'll make you another dress." But Kerry shook her head.

"If we don't find it, I'll wear something else—anything. But I shall marry Garth—nothing shall keep me from marrying Garth."

Kerry knew Trix would go home and tell her husband and her family, and they would tell the others, and no one would be surprised. They had expected something to happen. Probably they would nod, look grave, and say this wasn't the end; this was only leading up to something worse.

She couldn't sleep. She was sure Miss Drury didn't either, and she wondered about Tim and Garth.

At a quarter to six she got up and dressed, and went downstairs. It wasn't quite light. She turned on the switches as she went, and when she came to the drawing-room for some reason she opened the door and looked in. Vaguely she realised she had been wondering how she could arrange the furniture so that the missing

105

writingdesk was less obvious.

She need not have bothered. The desk was back. So was the picture and the bowl of *pot pourri*. The room was exactly as Miranda had left it—as Miranda wanted it to be.

CHAPTER SEVENTEEN

Leaving the drawing-room wide open, Kerry went into the kitchen and began to cook the breakfast. They'd see the room as soon as they came down, and suddenly she felt helpless, as though there was nothing she could do.

Miss Drury was down next. Kerry heard her stop short at the drawing-room door and the moment's silence before her footsteps, heavier and slower, came towards the kitchen.

"It's back," she said.

"I know."

"The writing-table, Kerry, and the picture. They're back in their old places."

"I know. Look, sit down, have a cup of tea." She was surprised that her own voice was so calm. God knew she felt like breaking into a thousand pieces, but she sounded calm enough.

Then Garth and Tim came downstairs together. Garth walked into the kitchen to ask: "Did anyone hear anything in the night?"

Kerry shook her head. Miss Drury said: "No."

Tim said: "We wouldn't have heard from upstairs, unless a great deal of noise was made."

"Did anyone move them back?"

Nobody spoke. They all shook their heads.

He held out a hand to Kerry and she clutched it, feeling

as though a rope was thrown to her in a quagmire. Garth's hand was strong, his pulse beat slowly, surely. "Come with me," he said.

He closed the drawing-room door behind them and stood still, holding her hand, looking down at her. "Do you want those things moved again, Kerry? Taken a long way away? Destroyed?"

"Would it help?" The way she felt now, she almost believed that if they had lit a fire in the courtyard last night and burned Miranda's things everything would still have been in place again this morning.

"I don't know."

"Garth, *is* she dead? She was never found."

"I wondered that for a long time. I think she could have played a trick like this for a while, but not for more than a year. She was angry when we parted. She wanted to hurt me and it would have amused her to frighten them all, but not all this time."

"Then how?"

"I wondered if Aunt Flora's behind some of it. She was very fond of Miranda but not insanely fond of her. When Miranda was alive they got on very well, but it's only since her death that Aunt Flora's developed this deep attachment. I think she feels that Miranda's must have been a deathless love."

"Do you?" She waited, afraid.

Garth said: "If Miranda's haunting me it isn't because of love, it's hate because I killed her," and before Kerry could protest: "I did and I know it, however it was done."

She tried to hold him close, but although she could feel his heart beating against hers she couldn't reach him. His eyes were brooding, dark with pain.

There was a tap on the door and Tim looked in. "What do you want us to do, Kerry?" he asked as Garth had

107

asked, and she said wearily:

"Nothing. Let it stay as it is."

It was less than a week to the wedding, and Aunt Flora and Kerry carried on with the preparations. They pretended that the wedding dress was still upstairs.

At least Kerry did. Before it disappeared she had felt a lift of the heart every time she walked into her bedroom and saw it there, even when it was only pinned and tacked together. Garth had never seen it and she had dreamed how he would look when she walked down the aisle to him. It had been a beautiful dress. Where was it now?

She and Miss Drury were in the kitchen icing the cake when she said bitterly: "It hardly seems worthwhile going to much trouble over a cake, does it? Not unless we intend to put a twenty-four-hour guard over it. Why shouldn't it go the way of the stole and the dress?"

"Of course it won't, child," Aunt Flora said, but her words were more reassuring than her voice.

"Do you think anyone will come to the wedding? They won't be scared?" Kerry asked her.

"They'll come. They're friends of Garth."

"Suppose we had cleared out her bedroom? Do you think that everything in that would have been put back, too? Suppose we do it this afternoon and watch tonight? Do you think we'd see her then?"

"Do you want to see her?"

She didn't know. Clare had seen Miranda, a slim figure with flying blonde hair, on the edge of the sea, but then Miranda had no hate for Clare. The girl who was to be her bridesmaid had never felt malevolence surrounding her like fog, woken up with a pillow smothering her face, almost stepped on the cotton reel at the top of the stairs.

Kerry knew she wouldn't try to clear Miranda's room, she wouldn't dare . . .

Clare came in the early afternoon and Kerry went out

to meet her. Clare had borrowed a little car, and she unloaded a couple of bottles of wine she had collected from the White Bear and reminded Kerry that they were all having dinner at Brenda's tonight.

Kerry did know, of course. Brenda had come over earlier in the week with a wedding present of some very beautiful coffee cups, and issued the invitation. But yesterday had shattered Kerry and now she didn't know whether she could face Brenda and Ginger, who so far as she knew had no idea of the things that were happening here.

She didn't feel like smiling or small talk, and from the appearance of her, neither did Clare. She still looked sick and Kerry said: "Have you seen Tim?"

"No, why?"

So she didn't know that the writing-desk was back. Kerry led the way into the hall and opened the drawing-room door.

"Oh God! Who did it?" Clare cried.

"That's how it was this morning."

They went back to the kitchen and tried to talk about other things, but the silences grew longer and Miss Drury made no attempt to fill them. She sat with a piece of embroidery, stitching small neat stitches.

Kerry said suddenly: "Shall we walk down and see Shirley?" She felt that she must get out of the house, even for only a few minutes.

Claire said: "I'll run you into town if you like. My mother said she hadn't seen you for days. That'll be all right won't it, Aunt Flora? We'll be back around six."

As they drove along the coast, Beth Lovelace came striding towards them and waved.

Clare raised a hand and drove on.

"Aren't you stopping?" Kerry asked.

"Oh, you know Beth Lovelace. We'd be chattering for

hours.'' Clare didn't sound quite natural. It was hard to pinpoint it, but Kerry knew that Clare was keeping her from Beth, and had probably only suggested this run to keep her from Shirley.

She turned to face Clare. 'What goes on?''

"Mmmm?''

"I want to talk to Beth. She's standing in the middle of the road goggling at us. She expected you to stop.''

"She always does. These folk live in each other's pockets.''

"Please, I want to go back.''

Clare grimaced and kept driving. "I think we've had enough mysteries for a few hours. I reckoned you could do without another. I heard this one in the White Bear.''

"All right, what was it?''

"They all know about the dress vanishing, of course. Trix told them. And last night some of the men were out fishing. Nat Lovelace was one of them. When they got home this morning their wives told them about your dress and they told their wives that they'd seen something floating in the sea. They didn't manage to pick it up, they'd got their nets out and it floated just out of reach. But of course they're all sure it was your wedding dress.''

Kerry said nothing. She was silent until they were almost at Clare's home, and then she said: "You think it was that too, don't you?''

"It could have been a hundred things. It could—'' Under Kerry's steady scruntiny she faltered and bit her lip. "Oh, what's the use? Yes, I suppose I do.''

Clare's mother was delighted to see Kerry. She knew everything of course, but she didn't have to live with it and didn't really believe it. She gave them tea, home-made hot scones and jam, and asked about the presents and didn't mention the wedding dress.

It was nice being with her, and driving back Kerry

decided she was glad they were going to Brenda's tonight after all. Better to keep your mind off things if they were ugly and frightening.

She put on a lime green dress; Clare looked attractive in a beige coarse-knit with long sleeves and a small collar.

Brenda had done her visitors proud. The table was gleaming under glasses, silverware and candles, and the delicious smell of a chicken casserole in a spicy sauce came from the kitchen.

They ate and talked and laughed. Only once was there a silence, and that was when Brenda said: "I'm dying to see your dresses. I know you'll both look wonderful."

Kerry stared down at her plate; Garth said something and the talk slipped into another topic.

Dining like this by candlelight reminded Kerry of those first evenings she and Garth had spent together. When she had discovered that he wasn't married, she had felt that the gods were kind. If someone had whispered: "Miranda, poor drowned Miranda," she would have felt a chill of pity, but she would never have believed that a ghost could be more real than a living girl, more to be feared.

Brenda laughed and snapped her fingers. "Come back, Kerry! We all know what your thoughts are, but come back."

A week from today was Kerry's wedding. That was what Brenda meant, but Garth and Tim and Clare knew that her thoughts were more likely to be grave than gay.

After their meal they all sat round the fire and Ginger showed them some tricks. He spent a fair amount of money and quite a lot of leisure on this hobby of his. Tonight he had a new trick.

He did it well and they applauded warmly. He did several more for them, and then brought out the in-evitable pack of cards. "Choose a card. Don't tell me which. Kerry, you choose one." When she took one he said: "You did that beautifully. Have you ever assisted a conjurer before?"

It was part of the patter and his mouth fell open when Kerry laughed and said: "As a matter of fact I have. I worked with one in a cabaret show in a nightclub when his assistant fell ill. I learnt some of the tricks of the trade, if your're interested."

"The professional touch? You bet I'm interested! What sort of act did you do?"

Kerry's smile vanished. She was frowning now, a strained frown of concentration. She said, on a note of amazement: "I've just realised who Mr. Potts reminds me of."

CHAPTER EIGHTEEN

It sounded like a joke. They waited. Kerry turned to Garth. "You know, the flowerpot men at Shirley's. I told you that one of them reminded me of somebody. It was a man I saw in this nightclub. They said he was a regular customer. He owned a lot of dubious property in London."

"Poor Mr. Potts," said Clare. "He wouldn't be flattered."

"You don't understand. He *is* Mr. Potts. He doesn't walk the same way, he shuffles around and he smiles. But it is the same man—I'm quite certain."

Now they were puzzled and still waiting. She remembered more. She would have remembered right away when she first saw him if there had been the slightest thing to link them. Remembering the conjurer had triggered it off. "His name was Masterson and he was next door to a crook."

"You mean that?" Ginger sounded interested.

"I don't mean he'd been to prison, I don't think he had, but he was certainly in some dirty rackets. What is he doing down here, pretending to be an invalid? If he was ill, a man like that wouldn't come to a place like this. He'd go somewhere fabulous."

"You must be making a mistake," Tim said. "People can look very like one another, you know. This old boy could have a double."

"Wait a bit," said Garth. "There's Miss Lambert, too."

"Miss Lambert?" Ginger didn't look like the smiling amateur magician any more. He looked eager, his eyes keen. "Tell me about Miss Lambert."

"She's another guest," Kerry said. "She's a hypochondriac and she insisted that Shirley should fire me because I have the wrong vibrations."

Brenda giggled, but Ginger said: "Any more?"

"One day I saw her taking a phone call and she didn't see me. She walked normally, looked about twenty years younger and she sounded quite different."

"Did you hear the call?"

"It was in a foreign language. Why?"

"Anyone else staying there?"

"Mr. Potts's brother."

"You're sure about Potts?"

"Quite sure. I wonder if he recognised me. He saw me two or three times."

"And Miss Lambert had you thrown out."

It might mean nothing, but it certainly sounded odd. Ginger had been squatting in front of Kerry, sitting on his heels. He got up now and did a couple of lengths of the room. Then he said: "Would you come down to the station and let the sergeant hear about this?''

''If you think I should.''

She didn't know what they were getting into, but she did realise it couldn't be left. She looked at Garth and he nodded a little reluctantly. ''You'll have to, darling.''

They left Clare and Tim and Brenda in a hushed group and took Ginger's car.

The sergeant at the station knew Garth. He looked up and grinned. ''Running him in, are we?''

''Not this time. It's just something we think you should hear,'' said Ginger, and they all sat down while Kerry told him.

He frowned, tapping a pencil to some rhythm of his own. At the end he said: ''You couldn't be mistaken about Mr. Potts?''

''He is Mr. Masterson, but there's no law against that, is there?''

''None at all. Hang on a moment will you? Just a minute, Ginger.'' The two policemen went out of the room and Kerry turned to Garth.

''What are they doing? What's happening?''

''We'll know soon.''

They were back soon, another man with them, about the same age as the sergeant but with the unmistakable air of rank about him. He smiled at Kerry. ''I'm Inspector Yarrow and I'm very interested in what you've been telling us.''

Kerry was beginning to feel a little panicky. This was snowballing alarmingly. Exactly what did they think was going on at the Crow's Nest? She said: ''Why are you so interested?''

''Because two fakes aren't likely to be under the same roof unless they're planning mischief.'' The inspector took Ginger's chair and waved the sergeant into the other. ''And Polbryn is a very lonely place, isn't it? Now

114

what could be going on at Polbryn?''

He looked at the sergeant and they both nodded. The sea, thought Kerry. "Smuggling?" she said.

"Possibly, possibly." He beamed at her as though he was a teacher of a bright pupil and she the bright pupil. "But perhaps not the usual sort of merchandise. Not drinks or drugs or that sort of thing, I'd venture to guess."

His smile went. "I'm going to confide in you because you may have helped us a great deal and there's a chance you're going to help us even more. Quite a little problem these days is illegal entry. You know what that is, of course?"

Coming into the country without a passport. Men and women who would not be allowed in, if they applied in the normal way, so they find a back door and slip in through it.

Garth said: "Do you think that's been going on?"

"Certainly it's been going on, and our coastline's a near-perfect spot for it. Lonely, impossible to patrol adequately, every bay shielded from the next. I'm not saying that the two beauties at this guest house are running anything like that, but it could be a sweet little racket for them."

Garth said slowly: "If they were, there's a cove that the villagers won't go near. It's supposed to be haunted."

Satisfaction spread over the inspector's face. He was rather thin-faced, but he smiled so broadly that he looked round and plump and jolly. "Couldn't be better!" he exclaimed.

Miranda's cove! Even Miranda's ghost if someone wanted to give the place a reputation of evil, bad luck.

"We ought to tell Shirley and Roland," Kerry said. "They could be in danger if the Potts brothers and Miss Lambert really are crooks."

"Shirley? Roland?" The inspector waited for her to elaborate.

"They run the guest house. They own it."

He nodded. "In that case, they're the last people we want to tell."

"What?" She knew what he meant, but she wouldn't accept it.

"Use your commonsense. If their house is the head-quarters, they're going to know. They've got to cooperate."

"No!" She twisted in her chair. "Garth, tell him they can't be. You've known them all your life."

"I've known them for years," agreed Garth. "Trelawney settled here about ten years ago. I'd stand surety for him."

For a moment the inspector looked almost sympathetic. Then he said: "It isn't a philanthropic set-up you know. They're not helping anyone except themselves. The folk they bring in are mostly honest and hard-working but coming in this way they're mortgaging their future. They'll be found homes—in Masterson's slums paying top prices. Work for him too, maybe, and if the jobs are underpaid they daren't complain. They shouldn't be here. A telephone call and the police would be around, and they'd be deported."

"But that would get the people who brought them in into trouble," said Kerry. "They'd be giving themselves away, too."

"Oh, no. These folk don't know where they're landed. They're whisked away as soon as they set foot on dry land. They see no one who matters or who they're likely to contact again. Believe me, it's very highly organised and it's the nearest thing to the slave trade still running. They're going to be blackmailed for the rest of their life."

116

She said miserably: "You know nothing for sure. It might only be coincidence about Miss Lambert and Potts."

He agreed. "But coincidences have to be investigated. You used to work at this place, you're still friendly with the owners?"

"Of course."

"Then would you be willing to go back there and keep your eyes open?"

"I can't go back."

"Just as a friend. Just calling in."

"No. I can't spy on them. I don't think Shirley and Roland have anything to do with this."

"All right, help us to prove that. Go and tell them what you've told me, that you recognise Masterson."

"Just a moment," said Garth. "That could be dangerous."

"Yes," agreed the inspector. "If they're innocent they'll be interested and surprised. If they're not they'll realise that this yound lady could be the wedge that splits their racket wide open."

"No." Garth's voice was very firm.

But Kerry said: "I'll do it."

The inspector beamed at her. "We'll watch the cove, of course, but that could be a long and risky job. We don't know when they're coming or where for sure. It would be better if we could blow the works at the source."

Kerry nodded. Garth said: "She isn't going into that house alone to tell them everything. If Potts is Masterson, you can work from there but Kerry isn't going to run into danger."

"She wouldn't be alone, and it wouldn't be just us behind her. You see, a backdoor way into the country is a gap in our defences. Others can come in besides the ones who only want to work and be left alone. Spies, saboteurs. Men and women who want to destroy us. This won't be my pigeon. Even on the little you've told me I'll have to hand it over to the men who specialise in this work. Can you be here in the morning, miss? I'm sure I don't have to ask you not to mention this to anyone.''

Perhaps she wasn't alone but she felt it when she knocked on the door of the Crow's Nest the next day. In her handbag was something that looked like a tiny black box and somehow it meant that a couple of men sitting in a Post Office repair van by a telegraph pole opposite could hear every word.

She wasn't proud of what she was trying to do. Shirley had been kind, and a good friend, and Kerry couldn't believe that she and Roland were involved in this sort of heartless work.

Shirley smiled when she saw her. "Hello, surprise! Come in.''

In the kitchen Roland was peeling potatoes and Shirley had been halfway through the washing-up. It was such an ordinary scene that Kerry felt her spirits rise.

"I've come to tell you about Mr. Potts. I've remembered where I saw him,'' she said.

They were both looking at her, and it was no imagination that the atmosphere was suddenly as tense and taut as a violin string.

CHAPTER NINETEEN

Where?'' said Shirley after those few electric seconds. Her voice was light, interested.

Kerry told them.

"I don't think so," said Roland. "Maybe he just looks like this Masterson."

"And Miss Lambert," Kerry went on. "She's hiding something, isn't she? They're both pretending to be something they're not."

"Doesn't everyone?" said Shirley. "It's no business of ours."

"I think you should tell the police."

"Kerry love," Shirley laughed and Kerry would have laughed with her had she not been alert and looking for other things—the way Shirley's hands gripped and her eyes narrowed. "Do you want to get this place a bad name? Have you told anyone else this?"

"I only remembered last night, but I'm sure Garth will agree that you ought to tell the police about Masterson, to cover yourselves."

Roland and Shirley looked at each other. He spoke in a strangely harsh voice: "I said you were a fool to have anyone else in the house. Betsy was as dim as a bat, but when you stopped her coming you should have left it at that."

"Should I?" snapped Shirley. "And work myself into the ground, I suppose. How was I to know she was going to recognise him? It's a big world. All right, go and get them."

Roland went. Kerry said: "What's going on here?"

Shirley sighed. "You little fool! Why did you have to do it? Why couldn't you mind your own business? No, stay where you are!" She picked up the short, sharp potato knife, and seconds later they all came clattering down the stairs.

Elvira Lambert had left her shawls behind and the Potts brothers had left their smiles.

"So it happened," said Miss Lambert. "She remembered What do we do with her now?"

119

"I think we all know that," said the man Kerry knew as Masterson.

"So you are all in some crooked game," Kerry said rather wildly and looked at Shirley and Roland.

They said nothing, but Roland gripped her, one hand came over her mouth. Although she knew that the doorbell would ring soon, her heart was beating suffocatingly.

"The question is—how?" Masterson said.

"The cove?" That was Roland.

"No. We don't want any more attention drawn to that right now. Don't forget tomorrow night's shipment. It has to look like an accident."

He didn't sound as though he considered it much of a problem.

Shirley's voice came shakily: "They'll think Miranda did it. They've been waiting for the last couple of months for Miranda to kill her."

Briskly, insistently, the doorbell rang.

Only Beth Lovelace saw them go. One of the cars passed her as she cycled along and she waved, glimpsing Shirley.

But Shirley did not wave back. She sat, stiff and expressionless, staring straight ahead.

Beth told everyone afterwards: "She looked so strange. As if she was sick or something."

The Crow's Nest was closed and shuttered. Plain-clothed silent men stood at doors, and the village could talk and think about nothing else.

Garth and Tim and Kerry and Clare said nothing. Soon this was going to make page-one headlines with the name of Polbryn splashed in every newspaper, but now silence and deep security shrouded it.

At present no one else knew that Elvira Lambert, that eccentric old invalid, was the brains behind an illegal entry combine, with the Mastersons her colleagues and henchmen. Or that the Crow's Nest had been their headquarters, and Shirley and Roland the respected front.

There was talk of shouts that had been overheard from the direction of the cove. Kerry remembered Masterson saying: "Don't forget tomorrow night's shipment," and knew that a boat without lights, with a muffled engine, had landed men and women on the wet shingle. Then the shadows had moved and they had found themselves surrounded.

Most of the cargo had been pathetic dupes but among them were the dangerous and the deadly. Now no more silent, darkened boats would come under cover of night to Miranda's cove.

They mystery of the Crow's Nest pushed Kerry's wedding into the background, except at Norbrook Farm. There, Aunt Flora said: "There was trouble about those guests of theirs, wasn't there?" and nodded as though she realised they knew more than they were allowed to tell.

Kerry was thankful that she had her love and her wedding to fill her mind; she would have hated to dwell on Shirley and Roland.

These days Miranda's scent was so strong that sometimes it made Kerry's head swim. The house seemed full of it, so that everyone who came in noticed it and exchanged glances with Miss Drury. Not with Kerry. They never spoke of it to her.

The scent—and Miranda's weather. It was stormy the day before the wedding, clouds were heavy. Kerry wished they would break because there were only a few hours left. If the storm didn't come today, it might break over tomorrow's wedding.

When Garth came in with Neil and Tim, she told him: "There are lots of parcels to be opened."

Garth smiled. "How does one girl make so many friends? No, don't tell me. I know when I look at you."

"Clare not here yet?" asked Tim. "She's going to get caught in the storm."

No one said, "Miranda weather," but they all thought it.

Clare was coming to stay the night, although tomorrow she wouldn't have to help the bride dress in a shimmering white gown. Kerry wasn't deciding until tomorrow what she'd wear. She would take something from her wardrobe and say: "I'll marry Garth in this."

Now she went with him into the dining-room. "One more toaster," she said, "and we can set up in business."

He grinned.

He had a very small parcel in his hand. Kerry said: "What's that?"

He took off the wrapping and disclosed a small box. Intrigued, hand on his shoulder, Kerry waited for him to open it, and lift up the cottonwool. The ring was an emerald, green and square.

She couldn't look at his face, only at the ring. She whispered: "Miranda's?"

He nodded.

"Then how—? Who sent it?" She picked up the paper it had been wrapped in but there was no writing on it.

"She was wearing it when she died."

Kerry had never fainted in her life but darkness suddenly swooped so that she swayed and felt Garth's arm around her.

"She didn't die, Garth. If this ring is here, she can't be in the sea."

All around her the perfume was powerful, enveloping. There was rain on the window, the kind of night Miranda loved. Perhaps she was out there now, behind the dark glass, watching them.

"It can't go on like this!" Kerry's voice was desperate.

"I know it," said Garth.

"She's dead." Kerry's doubts had been only momentary. "We know she's dead and she must leave us alone. Whether she hates you or loves you she must go away."

Garth still held the emerald ring. It was very like the one that Kerry had almost chosen.

"How much did you love her?" Kerry asked.

"Not like I love you." At last he had said it. "Nothing like that. It was probably because I'd saved her life and I was sorry for her. It made a bond between us."

"How much did she love you?"

He smiled a little grimly. "A fair amount, I think. She wanted to marry me, but if I'd been a poor man I doubt if she would have."

"You could be penniless, it would make no difference to me. If everyone in the world was against you, and I knew that loving you meant I should be an outcast for the rest of my life, I'd still love you."

"And I you." He held her hands and she felt the pressure of Miranda's ring.

The storm had broken, was crashing around them, and Kerry said: "Do you think she's out there?"

"I don't know."

"The police think the girl that was seen in the cove was Shirley, that she was frightening people away? But it isn't Shirley here, and Shirley didn't send this ring. Miranda's got to listen to us somewhere. Perhaps on the cliffs, tonight."

She was on her feet, dragging him with her. She would have run out into the rain as she was, coatless, hatless, if he hadn't picked up two raincoats as they went through the hall.

123

Did she really feel that Miranda might be waiting for them? Kerry only knew that the time for turning away was over.

CHAPTER TWENTY

Faces streaming with water, they reached the little shelter of stones. It was some protection against the storm and the rain. The night was so dark that you could hardly see the waves beneath. But you could hear them as they howled.

Kerry turned to face Garth. "You stood here with her?"

"Yes."

"You quarrelled and you left her."

"Or I killed her."

"No," she said again, and again he said:

"You don't understand. I was almost sure there was another man and she told me there had been, but it was over now. I was angry because she said it was Tim."

"Tim?" The name jerked from her.

"It wasn't true. I knew that, but all the same I could have killed her."

Kerry held him close and called into the wind: "Miranda, can you hear us? Please let us alone and let us live our lives. We love each other."

No answer came except from the wind, the sea and the rain.

"Garth," Kerry cried, "you tell her."

He spoke into the darkness. "I love you, Kerry. I never loved any woman as I love you, and I shall love you until I die."

There was a movement beside them. A man stepped from the shadows, and spoke in a hoarse voice: "You can't love anyone but Miranda. You mustn't stop loving her."

The rain streamed from him.

"Neil." Garth's voice was quiet. "So you were the man."

Neil Pontin didn't seem to have heard. He grabbed Garth by the lapels of his coat, and his face was intense and purposeful. "You can't marry anyone else," he said.

Garth said gently: "Miranda's dead, Neil. It doesn't matter."

Kerry thought, they should be shouting, screaming, anything except facing each other so quietly, their voices so calm.

"I know her better than any of you because I loved her more," Neil said. "For a little time she even loved me."

"You've been keeping her alive?"

He turned away, towards the sea. "She didn't want to die. She loved life. You remember how she loved life? And Norbrook, too. She's told me many times that she'd never leave it. I did the things she'd want done. I kept her there."

Kerry saw it all so vividly now—Neil walking through the old house, his step quick and light, opening a door, replacing a picture, tearing a stole to shreds.

"My wedding dress?" she said suddenly.

"I threw it into the sea. It was like giving it to her. When I heard she'd been seen in the cove I thought—I must keep Norbrook the way she wants it.

"So I put things back in place. When Miss Drury first saw a vase put back she stood and stared at it, then she whispered: 'Miranda.' Just the name, and it was like calling her." Neil was talking quickly now. "You'd have forgotten her if it hadn't been for me. Not completely,

125

but she would have been pushed to the back of your minds. I saw that she wasn't.

"The perfume helped. I'd got a big bottle made up as a present for her, but I didn't have time to give it to her. When I was at Norbrook I'd put a little on curtains, cushions, places like that. And later if I walked into a room and smelt it—she was there for me."

Kerry said wonderingly: "Did you try to kill me?" and as Garth turned sharply: "Things happened, I thought Miranda hated me."

"She would have," said Neil. "She'd have hated you enough to kill you if you'd married Garth."

Garth caught him savagely now. "What did you do to Kerry?"

"I only wanted to frighten her. I wouldn't have hurt her."

"I believe that," she said quietly. They had only been threats, they might have driven her away.

"The ring?" Garth asked tautly. "Miranda was wearing it when I left her that night."

"Yes."

"You saw her afterwards. You must have been here when she went over the cliff."

"Yes," said Neil. "But I didn't kill Miranda."

"What happened?"

"When she came up here, when it was stormy, I came, too. Often she'd send me away, but sometimes she'd let me stop with her. I was here that night. I heard you quarrelling. I heard her tell you about Tim. She was lying. I suppose you knew, but you were angry and you went away."

Garth closed his eyes for a fleeting moment, and Kerry thought—thank God. He'll never look at his hands again and wonder if they killed Miranda.

"I asked her why she did it," Neil was saying, "and

she laughed and said she loved making you angry."

"And then?" prompted Garth.

"She knew I loved her. I'd never really thought there was a chance for me, I knew I should marry Lissy one day and try to make her a good husband, but Miranda was—well she was a sort of dream.

"I'd told her that, often. She liked to hear it. Sometimes she'd say she was in love with me. It was the same that night. I made a fool of myself. I said we'd go away from here and I'd get a job as a photographer and she took the ring off her finger. She gave it to me. She put it in my hand and at first I thought she meant it and was coming with me. But she said: 'Buy me another as big as that and then I might think about leaving Garth.'

"I said, 'You don't know what you want,' and she said, "Oh yes I do. I want Garth and Norbrook and all that money.'

"I meant to throw the ring over the cliff. She could do that, make you so angry that you hardly knew what you were doing. I raised my hand and she thought I'd thrown it and she darted forward wildly."

Now there was no expression at all in Neil's face. "She went over the edge. She screamed once and then she was just foam on the sea. And I ran. I don't know where. Along the cliffs. There was nothing I could do. I ran and I wanted to die."

The storm was leaving them. Lightning still flashed over the dark water, but the thunder came seconds later.

"I found the ring in my pocket," Neil went on. "I must have automatically slipped it in when I ran along the cliff. I put it in a drawer and never looked at it again until today. I couldn't bear to touch it. Miranda died plunging after that damned thing."

Kerry felt an overwhelming pity. Neil had always seemed so dull and contented. No one had suspected the

127

loneliness he carried, or that he was trying to atone to Miranda by keeping her alive.

He said now: "They've seen her in the cove. I had nothing to do with that. So she has come back."

"That wasn't Miranda," said Garth. "Believe me, it wasn't. I have proof that it was Shirley in the cove—Shirley they saw."

Neil had faced the storm, head up. Now his head bowed until he was holding it in his hands, like a man in pain. His voice was muffled. "Then she never came back?"

"No."

"I thought I owed her—"

"You owed her nothing," said Garth. "She died by accident."

Kerry thought: Lissy will help him. If he tells her she'll help him.

Neil stood still. As Garth touched him, Neil asked: "What are you going to do?"

"We'll talk later." Garth held out the emerald ring and looked at Kerry.

She took it from his hand and threw it in a wide arc down into the sea. It was Miranda's ring. She had wanted it enough to die for it.

Garth nodded. "Now let's go home."

Neil Pontin walked a little ahead of them. The storm was over, and with Garth's arm around her Kerry felt the past was over, too. Her heart light, she went home to wait for tomorrow and her wedding day.

THE END

AC/4200-26/P171